End of Secrets

Book Seven of the Vital Secrets Series

D.F. Hart

2 of Harts Publishing
WWW.2OFHARTS.COM

The Vital Secrets Series

End of Secrets

Visit 2ofharts.com to sign up for my newsletter and get a special bonus supplement to the series!

Follow me on:
BookBub
Goodreads
Facebook

Custom Cover Design and Artwork commissioned for D.F. Hart by:
Rocking Book Covers
Handcuffs graphic by Adam Lapunik of Vecteezy.com

Published 2022 by 2 Of Harts Publishing
Arlington, Texas

For Anita—

Without whose support and encouragement this series might never have gotten past book two.

Things fall apart; the center cannot hold.

—Yeats

That's the problem with secrets. Some of them are too dangerous to reveal—and others are too dangerous to keep.

—Nathan Thomas

Chapter One

FOUR WEEKS HAD PASSED since FBI Agent Ben Tinsing's coldblooded murder, and his boss, Nathan Thomas, woke up once again covered in sweat.

Trembling, he sat up and glanced over at the alarm clock.

Two-forty-two a.m.

He ran his hands over his face, then back through his hair before he pulled back the covers. Beside him, he heard Bella sigh and felt her roll from her back to her side. He paused, listening, and once he was certain she was still sleeping, he got out of bed as quietly as he could.

He grabbed his cell phone from its charging station on the nightstand and took it with him as he left the bedroom, moving down the dark hallway to the kitchen to start the coffeepot.

While he waited for his first cup of what he knew in his core would be fuel for an exceptionally long day, he glanced at his phone and noticed he'd missed a text from DEA Agent Hank Myers a little after eleven the night before.

I'll be back in Dallas this week. Thought we'd grab lunch. Have some updates for you.

Sounds good, Nathan typed in reply, then set the phone down to retrieve a mug from the cabinet.

The ping of a new message startled him.

Can't sleep either, huh? Hank asked.

Nope, not much at all lately, Nathan typed back.

"And I'm not sure I ever will again," he muttered to himself as he filled his mug, then headed back down the hallway to the bathroom for a shower.

In Tulsa, a restless Annie Adams finally gave up any further attempts at sleep around five-fifteen. She sighed, threw back the covers, and stood.

Great. Now what?

As she reached for her robe the same conversation started up again in her head, but this time, she didn't deflect it as she had for the past month.

Where do I go from here?

She already knew on some level that her retreat to Tulsa was meant to be a respite, not a permanent relocation. She'd spent the time since her arrival reconnecting with her parents, and she was grateful for their love and their unconditional support.

But it didn't fill the void. Not by a long shot.

More worrisome, lately the grief that surrounded her like a dark cloud had become increasingly rage-filled, as well.

She wanted closure.

No, not closure, her inner voice immediately corrected in a steely tone. *Retribution.*

And I can't do it from Tulsa, she realized. *I cannot just run away and hide from my life forever.*

Deep in thought, she slipped on her robe and left her room, and as she padded down the carpeted stairs, Annie sighed again.

She took the last step down to the first floor, turned right to walk into the bright and airy kitchen, and was surprised to see her father already sitting at the table with the day's newspaper.

"Morning, sunshine. You're up early."

"Hey, Daddy. Yeah, couldn't sleep so I figured I might as well get out of bed."

He folded his paper and set it aside.

"Want to talk?"

She shrugged.

"Come on, Annie-bug," he coaxed, and patted the seat next to him. "Let's talk it out."

She smiled at the loving nickname and joined him at the table.

"Let me guess. Trying to figure out if you should go back," he said gently.

She leaned over to rest her head on his shoulder.

"Not just that," she confessed. "I'm trying to figure out if I even still want to *be* an agent, Daddy."

"Do you like what you do?"

"Yes, very much."

"Then you should keep doing it. Ben would want that for you, honey."

"I know. I just... I don't know if I can, Daddy. I don't know if I can handle being back there. So many memories..."

He wrapped an arm around her in silent understanding.

"But at the same time, I've just got so much *anger*. You know? And I feel like unless we find Ben's killer and put him away, I will never be able to let that anger go."

"Makes sense. And from what you've shared with your mom and me, you have a great group of teammates, Annie. You don't have to do any of this on your own," her father pointed out.

"True," she admitted.

"Then it sounds to me like you already know what you need to do, kiddo."

She sighed once more.

"Yeah. I do. I need to get back to Dallas."

He squeezed her shoulders.

"Let me know when you're ready and I'll help you load the car, Annie-bug. In the meantime, want to help your old man whip up some breakfast?"

Up in Seattle, Hank Myers finished packing, then checked his watch.

It took ten trips down to his truck to load it all, after which he made one last trip through the furnished apartment he'd called home for three years to ensure he'd left nothing behind.

He locked the door for the last time, worked the key off his keyring, sealed it in the envelope he'd prepared, and trudged down to the complex's office to slip it through the mail slot.

The moment the envelope left his grasp, he felt something wash over him that he never expected – an overwhelming sense of freedom, like the last wisp of web entangling him had melted away.

Grinning in surprise, Hank returned to his parking space and climbed into his truck.

"Twin Falls, Idaho. That sounds like a good place to stop for the night," he murmured aloud as he logged his ultimate destination of Pantego, Texas into his GPS, then looked at the map that showed the most efficient route.

He started his truck, backed out of the parking space, and pulled out of the lot and into the waking dawn.

As he made his way onto I-90 East to begin his 2,100-mile pilgrimage, his mind drifted, recalling the past four weeks that had been the hardest of his life.

He'd left Dallas after Ben Tinsing's funeral service to head straight into another grief-filled event – escorting Cruz Delgado's remains home for burial.

The time he'd spent back home in Del Rio, Texas had almost been a blur; he'd reinforced his walls to try to keep the pain from eviscerating him as he'd upheld the promise he had made long ago to his best friend.

But seeing Cruz's parents again and hearing their wails of sorrow had pierced through to his soul, and in Cruz's brothers' eyes he saw the same heavy grief that threatened to drown him.

He'd stayed long enough to watch as his friend's casket was lowered into the earth. But the distinctive sound of freshly turned soil drumming steadily against Cruz's coffin as the hole was filled in was too much. Hank had abruptly turned on his heel, walked to his rental car parked along the thin strip of pavement adjacent to Cruz's final resting place, and fled.

When he returned to Seattle, he felt restless and unanchored. Hank spent the following two weeks in solitude, and he'd returned to work the week after that.

He'd no sooner walked into his office when the power-hungry branch director immediately summoned him to a disciplinary session.

Hank sat across from the man, who began the meeting by announcing Hank's formal reprimand for daring to travel to Dallas to search for Cruz without prior clearance. The more the director spoke, the less of a damn Hank gave, until he finally reached his limit.

The smirk Hank wore as he stood, loudly announced his immediate resignation, and slammed his badge and his agency-issued weapon on his boss's desk grew into a wide, satisfied smile when he saw the man's stunned and panicked expression.

After that, he'd gone back to his apartment and made some calls to further develop the seeds of an idea that quitting the DEA had sown in his mind.

And now? Hank thought as he cranked up the radio and drove toward the rising sun.

Now, I'm free to chase my future.

"Hey girl," Lizzie Zimmerman said when she answered the phone a little before nine a.m.

"Hey Lizzie," Annie replied. "I need a favor."

"Name it."

"I'm coming back, and I need a place to crash for a few days until I get my living arrangements lined out. I'd ask Grace but she's on that cruise this week."

"Like you even have to ask me. Get yourself to my house, Annie. You're welcome to stay as long as you need to."

"Thanks, I appreciate it. Should be there by five."

Lizzie disconnected the call and glanced over at Donny, who was in the process of bringing a stack of pancakes and the syrup over to the table.

"I don't mind at all, you know that," he reassured his wife, knowing by her expression what she was about to ask him. "Because I know that Annie is more than your co-worker, Liz. She's part of your *family*."

Lizzie grinned.

"Yes, she is. Guess I'd better go make sure the guest bedroom is ready for her."

"Not before you let me feed you, you're not. Pancakes are better warm."

In Reynosa, Mexico, Estoban Cortinas' top henchman paused outside his master's bedroom door and mentally braced himself for the impending storm, then took a deep breath and knocked loudly.

"*What?*" came the surly snarl.

"Your father, Patrón. He's sent a car for you."

The man held his breath and waited, steeling himself not to flinch when the door was flung open and a furious Estoban stared him down.

"He thinks to *summon* me, like some commoner off the street?" Estoban growled.

The man shrugged his shoulders nonchalantly as he held Estoban's stare. But his sharp gaze noticed the subtle traces of white residue under his boss's nose that confirmed he'd jump-started his day once again with chemicals.

"We'll see about that. Dismiss the car. Tell them I'll go visit with dear old Papa when I'm good and ready," Estoban intoned, his face scarlet with anger as he stepped back into his sanctuary once more.

"Yes, Patrón," came the neutrally toned reply as Estoban slammed the door as hard as he could in the man's face.

As the man newly appointed by Silvadore Cortinas himself to protect the cartel king's oldest son walked away to do Estoban's bidding, he could clearly hear the tempest of destruction raging behind the closed door.

He stepped back into the front foyer to relay Estoban's message to Silvadore's personal driver and kept his expression purposefully blank as he watched the chauffeur gulp at the news.

Estoban's coke habit is out of control, and he is becoming more unstable by the day, he acknowledged silently as the nervous driver left empty-handed.

He moved swiftly into a room just off the foyer, closed the door behind him, and pulled his cell phone from his pocket. With a deep exhale, he dialed, and waited.

Once he'd finished trashing everything within easy reach, Estoban Cortinas snorted two new lines, then paced back and forth in his debris-filled bedroom and struggled to tuck his rage back into its box for safekeeping.

How dare he send a car for me, like I'm some nobody, he fumed as he paced.

He was on his fourth circuit when he stopped abruptly, and his lips curved into a feral smile.

Time to pay the old man a visit – on my *terms.*

A determined Estoban wheeled around and marched through his destroyed bedroom to take a shower and line out his plans.

***

An hour away, in Matamoros, cartel head Silvadore Cortinas hung up the phone and frowned.

He picked up the perfectly prepared cup of coffee that his butler had brought to him and strolled across the study of his sprawling, luxurious estate to sit by the fireplace and contemplate the difficult road ahead.

Perhaps I should have done this sooner, he thought to himself as he sipped, then watched the flames dance in a hypnotically soothing rhythm.

He is my firstborn son, and I love him. But I can no longer stay my hand because of it.

***

By eleven, Annie's car was loaded to the brim once more, and she hugged both her parents tightly one last time before she walked to her car to climb behind the wheel.

"Call when you get there so we don't worry," her mom prompted, and she nodded.

"I will. I love you both," she announced.

"And we love you. We're here if you need us, Annie-bug," her dad said. "Drive carefully."

***

As Annie pulled out of her parents' driveway in Tulsa, Hank Myers passed the city limit sign for Baker City, Oregon and took the first exit to find lunch and gas. A half-hour later he resumed his trek southeast.

After Lizzie made sure the guest room was set up and ready for Annie's arrival, she made herself comfortable on the couch to spend a lazy Sunday of watching television with Donny.

When her cell phone rang a little before one, she glanced at it, then answered.

"Hey, boss, what's up?"

"Hi," Nathan responded. "I need to pick your brain. Can you come over?"

"Sure, I guess. What's up?"

"Well," Nathan managed before yawning, "I'm looking at some stuff Steve sent down, and I could use another set of eyes on it."

"You sound exhausted," she murmured. "You all right?"

A long pause followed her question before she finally heard him say, "It is what it is, Lizzie. See you in twenty?"

"On my way," she confirmed.

She hung up the phone and looked at Donny, whose eyebrow had raised with curiosity.

"He doesn't sound good," she volunteered.

"It doesn't surprise me, to be honest," Donny told her. "You of all people know how seriously he takes his team's safety. That's been breached now, and it weighs on him."

"Danger is just part of the job," Lizzie sighed. "He can't keep punishing himself for what happened to Ben. He couldn't have known things would go like that, much less prevent it. But I know Nathan, and yes, he's taking it as a personal failure."

"So, talk to him, Liz. He'll listen to you."

She smiled and leaned over to kiss Donny before she stood up.

"I'd already planned to."

When Lizzie arrived, Bella was waiting at the front door for her.

"I thought you and I could talk for just a moment."

"Sure."

"I'm worried about him, Lizzie," Bella confided softly, and Lizzie could plainly see and hear the strain she was under. "He doesn't realize that I am aware of it, but he hardly sleeps anymore, and the little bit of rest he does get isn't peaceful. He tosses and turns and wakes up shaking and covered in sweat."

"Has he talked to anybody?"

Bella shook her head.

"No, not yet. But he needs to. It's the hospital explosion all over again, Liz."

Lizzie reached over and squeezed her hand.

"I'll try, Bella. That's all I can promise."

"I know, and I appreciate it."

They turned and began to walk through the living room when a blur of movement caught Lizzie's eye.

"Hey, little buddy," she said with a grin as she scooped up Charlie, who had run at her full tilt.

"Hi Izzy," he replied with a toothy grin before he flung his arms around her neck to hug her. "Watch cartoons?"

"I can't right now, kiddo. I came over to help your dad with something. Maybe later, okay?"

He huffed and responded, "Kay."

"It's lunchtime, Charlie. Chicken nuggets and mac and cheese," Bella informed him, and Charlie wriggled out of Lizzie's arms to race into the kitchen.

His mother looked over at Lizzie and smiled.

"Works every time. Go on back, Liz, he's in his office."

Lizzie walked down the hall and rapped on the open doorframe to get Nathan's attention.

"Hey, you. Need more coffee?"

He stood, stretched, and nodded.

"Always, how about you?"

"I could use a cup."

They walked back to the kitchen side-by-side.

"I made you a sandwich," Bella announced, and pointed to a plate on the counter.

"Thanks, honey," he said as he refilled his mug.

"Lizzie, you want one?" Bella offered.

"Just coffee for me at the moment, but thanks."

The two agents retreated to Nathan's office and settled in after Lizzie shut the door behind them.

"Before we get started on what Steve sent you, I'd like to talk for a bit," she said solemnly, and Nathan gestured for her to continue as he took a sip and set his mug down.

"You realize that what happened to Ben wasn't your fault, right?"

His brow furrowed.

"But," he started to say, but Lizzie held her hand up and stopped him from going further.

"No buts, Nathan. It wasn't an avoidable situation. And you didn't send Ben to go do transport. You asked for volunteers, remember? And he volunteered."

"I remember," he retorted as the muscle in his jaw began to twitch.

"No one knew what was going to happen. There's no way anyone could have predicted it."

"*But I should have!*" Nathan thundered and slammed both fists down hard on his desk. "I should have had my freaking head in the game more. We were running a full-court press against an extremely dangerous cartel, and I knew it, and I should have thought ahead and realized they'd try to get to Ramon to shut him up. But I didn't, and Ben paid for my mistakes with his life."

He scrubbed his hands over his face before he looked over at her with stormy, haunted eyes.

"I failed him, Lizzie. I failed him, and he's gone."

She held his grief-filled gaze as she leaned forward and took his hand.

"*None* of us thought about that, Nathan. None of us recognized that Ramon would be an active target at that point in time. Even the *directors* didn't, or they would have had way more than just two agents assigned to transport him. And do you know why?"

He frowned.

"Enlighten me."

"Because at the time we took him in, we thought we'd escaped detection, remember? Think about it. From what we all knew at the time, we'd picked him up without the cartel noticing anything. That was the whole reason we went after him at the restaurant and not the garage, to make sure that it went unnoticed. Right?"

Nathan nodded on a shaky exhale.

"Yeah, at the time, we thought we'd managed to fly under their radar," he admitted.

"So, they must have had someone watching Ramon, and whoever was tailing him was at the restaurant that night and saw us take him into custody. I've been racking my brain for the last month, and that's the only thing I can think of. Otherwise, they'd never have known about it - because we took steps to ensure that our plan to grab him was rock solid."

She paused and squeezed his hand.

"My point is, *none of us* realized that the cartel knew he'd even been arrested, much less by us, or that they would take steps to take him out. This was a perfect storm. None of what happened is your fault or your burden to carry, Nathan, and to say or think otherwise is not fair to you."

Lizzie released his hand and leaned back in her chair.

"And for the record, I've talked to Baker a few times now, and guess what? He doesn't blame you, either. He puts the blame where it belongs – on the cartel. So now the question becomes, can you lay this burden down? Because we need you, Nathan. We need you to lead this team. Ben's gone, and it's not fair. It sucks, and it hurts. But you did not cause this. *It is not your fault.*"

Nathan closed his eyes and lowered his head as her words washed over him, and she waited and watched him as he struggled within himself.

"Here's what I'd like to do," she offered softly. "I know we watched the restaurant's interior footage to help tie the noose around Ramon Gutierrez's neck for what he did to Annie. I want us to look at any *exterior* footage, whether it's the restaurant's or from other cameras in the area. I have a feeling that when we do, we're going to spot Ramon's tail carefully hidden somewhere in the background, and we can take steps to hunt down Ben's killer from there. You in?"

He lifted his head again, and she saw the raw rage shining in his eyes when he answered her.

"You bet your ass I'm in."

Annie hummed along with the radio as she drove through Pauls Valley, Oklahoma, heading south on I-35 toward the Texas border. With each mile that passed, she felt more certain that returning to Dallas was the right move.

Should I call Nathan first, or just show up at the office in the morning? she mused, and then remembered Lizzie talking about the time off she'd taken when her father had passed away.

I'll ask Lizzie when I see her. She'll know.

Her thoughts were derailed when the station she was listening to started to play a song that she knew all too well.

Too soon, she acknowledged as the opening notes of Ben's favorite song tore a fresh hole in her heart, and she quickly changed the channel with a trembling hand.

I don't know if I will ever be able to listen to it again.

The next two and a half hours seemed to last forever, and Annie finally heaved a sigh of relief as she pulled to the curb outside Lizzie's and Donny's house.

She'd barely made it out of her car before Lizzie was at her side gathering her into a hug.

"Welcome back, girl," she heard, and felt Lizzie patting her back as the tears flowed freely again.

After a few minutes, when she'd composed herself, she glanced over Lizzie's shoulder and noticed Donny smiling at her.

"Good to see you, Annie."

"Hi," she managed as Lizzie finally turned her loose, and she stepped back and wiped her eyes.

"Thanks. It's good to be back."

"What needs to be unloaded first?"

Annie shrugged.

"How about this," Lizzie countered. "Dinner first, *then* we'll get you settled in."

"Sounds like a plan."

Hank Myers rolled into Twin Falls, Idaho a little before six p.m. and drove around until he found a suitable hotel. He parked, grabbed his duffel bag from the front passenger seat, and made sure his truck bed's tonneau cover was locked before he went to the front desk to get a room for the night.

He let himself into his suite on the fifth floor, then headed for a shower to wash away the mild stiffness of being behind the wheel for nine hours. After that, he ordered room service and plotted out the next leg of his trip while he waited for his meal.

By nine p.m. he was sound asleep, with the room's standard issue alarm clock set for six in the morning.

Chapter Two

"Good to see you again, Annie," Nathan told her when he looked up and saw her standing in his doorway at the Dallas office on Monday morning.

"You too," she replied with a small smile as she entered and took a seat in one of his visitor's chairs.

"So, what's up?" he asked.

"I'm back," she said simply. "I'm glad I took that time away, but now I need to get back to work. We have a killer to catch."

"Agreed. In fact, Lizzie and I talked about a battle plan just yesterday afternoon."

"I know. She told me last night."

At Nathan's puzzled look, Annie explained.

"Grace isn't back from that cruise yet, and I didn't feel right staying over there without asking her first, so, I called Lizzie. I'm crashing at her and Donny's house until I can figure something out."

"Fair enough. I made some calls to try to round up some video for us to review. Hopefully, I'll have more news on that by the end of the day. We'll see."

"Anything you need me to start working on?"

"Actually, yes," Nathan said with a grin and handed over two files. "Go down to the lab and ask about the test results for these two cases. They'll be happy to see you. I know they've missed you, too."

She grinned back at him.

"You got it, boss. Be right back."

***

While Annie rode the elevator to go reunite with the lab techs, Hank Myers made excellent time traveling through Provo, Utah. He'd left Twin Falls early enough to beat the start of rush hour through Salt Lake City.

He'd selected Albuquerque, New Mexico as his next overnight stop – which meant a thirteen-hour day behind the wheel.

By all rights, he was on his own timelines – nowhere specific he had to be – and he'd taken his time and enjoyed the scenery between Seattle and Twin Falls.

But he'd jolted awake at four a.m. consumed with a sudden sense of urgency; the bone-deep *need* to get to Dallas quickly was almost overwhelming, and he had no idea what was driving it. All he knew was that for some reason being in Dallas as soon as possible was of the utmost importance.

He'd learned long ago to follow his gut instincts, and his years in the DEA had honed those instincts to a razor-sharp point. As a result, he'd only paused in the hotel's small dining room long enough to fill his travel mug with coffee and grab two donuts to take with him.

He was back on the road at four-sixteen.

Hank took another sip from his travel mug, set it back down in the cupholder, and whistled along with the radio as he continued his trek. As his GPS instructed, he left Interstate 15 in Spanish Fork to merge onto US-6 East, then US-191 South to continue his way toward the New Mexico state line.

"That was a good call, Lizzie," Nathan told her that afternoon as his team took their seats around the conference room table. "The restaurant owner's camera system deletes footage after forty days. We almost missed getting what we needed."

"What about other cameras in the area?" Annie asked softly.

"I had better luck with the ones operated by the city. Private sector, not so much. Most of those overwrite their recordings every month."

Nathan paused and sighed.

"Still, we have some good footage to work with. It's just a matter of wading through it."

"If it helps us figure out who took Ben from us, I'll watch footage all day every day," Annie announced, her jaw set.

"Absolutely," Nathan agreed solemnly, then picked up his cell phone as it vibrated and looked at the screen.

"Excuse me one moment," he said, and stepped out into the hall.

"Good afternoon, Hank," Nathan began as he answered the call. "How are you?"

"Headed your way," Hank replied in a clipped tone. "I'm about an hour from Cortez, Colorado. I'd like to meet with you when I get into town. Best guess is sometime Tuesday night or Wednesday morning."

Nathan frowned at Hank's tone.

"Something's wrong. What is it?"

"I'm not sure, Nathan. All I know is I need to be down there."

"Well, that's very... cryptic, Myers. Are you coming down on official DEA business, or can you not tell me that either?"

Nathan heard him snort out a laugh.

"Hardly. I'll explain more when I see you."

"Fair enough. Got a place to stay when you get into town?"

"Haven't thought that far ahead, to be honest."

"Come to my place, if you want."

"Roger that. I'll call you again when I'm about an hour out."

A confused Nathan hung up, shook his head, and returned to the conference room.

"Just so you know, Hank Myers is coming back into town," he revealed to his team once he'd retaken his seat at the table. "His ETA is sometime Tuesday night or Wednesday morning. We're supposed to meet up."

"How's he doing? I know Cruz's death was hard on him," Annie remarked.

"As far as I know, he's good. But you know Hank. Plays stuff close to the vest most days."

"Yeah. So, about that footage. Which one do you want me to take?"

"The restaurant. Lizzie, Mark, Herb, and I will start on the other recordings."

With the video files divided up between them, the team got to work – and it wasn't long before Annie paused her video and called out.

"Nathan, can we pull up one of the garage videos? I think I found something."

"Sure. Which one do you need?"

"Anything with Javier in it. I just noticed a guy outside the restaurant. I think it could be him."

"We never did get a clear shot of his face," he reminded her.

"I know. But I still think if we view the two images side-by-side we'll be able to rule him in or out," Annie said confidently.

Nathan cued up one of the videos they'd seized from the Fort Worth smuggling front and brought it up on the oversized drop-down screen, then repeated his efforts with the video Annie had been watching.

"Interesting. Same height and build, for sure," Lizzie noticed. "Zoom in?"

Nathan adjusted the feeds until two close-up still images appeared side-by-side.

"Can't be one-hundred-percent certain, but it looks like the same guy to me," Mark commented, and Herb nodded his agreement.

Lizzie swung her gaze from the oversized wall screen to Nathan.

"What does your famous gut say about it?"

There was a long pause before he replied.

"My gut says Javier watched us grab Ramon. It would explain how the cartel knew about it – and it would *also* explain why Javier wasn't at the garage the next day when we raided the place."

"I thought he was just a mechanic," Mark muttered.

"I did too," Nathan admitted. "But there's obviously more to him than we thought."

He paused and looked around the room at his team.

"The question is, how much more?"

The meeting wound down and as the others filed out, Lizzie gestured to Nathan to wait.

Once they had the space to themselves, she turned to him and said, "I think we need to continue reviewing that restaurant footage."

"What's your theory?" Nathan said, intrigued.

"I want to see how long this guy stuck around after we took Ramon into custody," she replied.

Nathan reached over and restored the restaurant footage to a full-screen view, then pressed 'play'.

Together, they watched as the mysterious figure they believed to be Javier hung back in the shadows, then climbed into a truck and followed the unmarked car that Ramon had been loaded into by Evans and Wilford.

"That's not good," Nathan muttered. "Not good at all. This guy watched the entire thing, Liz. Which means he'd be able to recognize *every team member we had on that operation...*"

He looked over at her.

"Get them back in here. *Now.* They need to know."

"On it," Lizzie said, and raced out the door to catch Mark, Herb, and Annie before they left the building.

As Lizzie left, Nathan reached over, picked up the conference room phone's handset, and dialed the director's extension.

"Sir, we have a problem. There's something you need to see."

He took advantage of the few minutes before the director's arrival to get Hank on the phone again and quickly share an abbreviated version of what they'd discovered.

After that, he pivoted to greet both his boss and the three team members that Lizzie had succeeded in finding and bringing back to the room.

"There's a new development, guys. Here's what we have," Nathan began, and played them the video.

"That's a good shot of the truck's license plate," the director pointed out, and Nathan dutifully captured a still image of the frame in question.

"Nathan," Lizzie said, "what do you think the chances are of seeing that same truck in the vicinity of *our* building on that same night?"

"At this point? I'd say high."

He turned to speak to his director, who waved him off.

"Already on it," Nathan's boss said as he pulled out his cell phone and called down to the building's security offices. "And I'll read in our DEA friends on the tenth floor, as well. They should know about this, since two of *their* agents were also in attendance that night."

Within the hour, they were looking at their office building's exterior footage on the night in question, and Nathan was dismayed to see the same truck come into view behind Ramon's transport car, then circle the block and park for a brief time.

"I think we need to go further," he said to the director. "I don't think whoever it was just gave up. They had to have come back and kept watch. How else would they have known when Baker and Ben left the building with Ramon?"

"My thoughts exactly – but I don't think waiting until morning and reviewing it with fresh eyes will hurt anything, do you?"

Nathan glanced at his team.

"No, sir," he said reluctantly. "I suppose not."

As Nathan's team in Dallas disbanded and a tired but determined Hank Myers pulled into a hotel parking lot up in Albuquerque, a smug Estoban Cortinas sauntered out into his Reynosa home's front foyer just after six p.m.

"You. With me," he commanded, and beckoned to his top man, then flicked his wrist toward his butler, who nodded and scurried to summon Estoban's car and driver.

When his bodyguard lifted an eyebrow, Estoban merely replied, "I think I've kept Papa waiting long enough, don't you?"

Nothing more was said until they were safely ensconced in the car and seated facing one another. Estoban nodded to the driver, who raised the partition to give them privacy before he navigated the limousine away from the front door and down the long, narrow driveway to the reinforced entry gate.

"I have a proposition for you," Estoban announced calmly, pinning his companion with a piercing stare. "And you will want to think very carefully before you answer."

"I'm listening."

"I know you're in my father's service, and that you currently answer to him," Estoban growled. "But I'm giving you one chance to prove your loyalty to *me*."

"What is it?"

Estoban told him, and he turned to look out the limousine's back window to confirm that two SUVs had fallen in line behind them.

The man was silent for a moment before responding, "Yes, Patrón, you have my word."

"Good answer," Estoban replied, "because it would have been a pity to ruin the car's upholstery."

He eased the handgun he'd been pointing at the man out of his pocket and into plain view, setting it down on the seat next to him.

"Now that that is settled, let's talk logistics."

Silvadore Cortinas had just taken his seat at the elegantly crafted mahogany dining room table for his evening meal when his butler reappeared at his elbow.

"Estoban is here," he was told, and he nodded.

"Show him in and set a place for him, please," Silvadore replied, and gestured to the chair to his left.

As his servant left to follow his instructions, the cartel boss sighed heavily once, and reached for his wineglass.

Well, at least we can eat together before I let him know what I've decided.

But the moment Estoban entered the room, Silvadore knew that the reports of his son's addiction had been severely understated. What he saw both shocked him and broke his heart.

Gone was the healthy complexion and the slight plumpness of the cheeks Estoban usually had, replaced with a paler, gaunt face with defined cheekbones. He also noticed a slight hand tremor as his oldest son walked toward him.

So much change in such a short time...

"Papa," Estoban murmured as he sauntered over to his place at the table and took his seat. "You summoned me?"

"Yes, I did - *yesterday morning*," Silvadore answered emphatically before he took another sip of his wine.

Estoban didn't bother to look ashamed, simply turned his focus to straightening his cufflinks.

"I wasn't able to come," he replied lazily with a wave of his hand. "Now, what did you wish to speak about?"

Silvadore cast a stony glare at his offspring - a look that usually brought his children to heel in an instant - and was dismayed to see that unlike before, his son not only didn't spring to attention, but yawned, as if bored.

Infuriated, Silvadore slammed down his glass.

"I had hoped to ease into this conversation, but your disrespectful attitude makes it plain that that is not possible," he snapped. "So, here it is – you're out. You've become a liability to me, so I'm replacing you as my second in command of the family business."

Estoban flung back his chair as he leapt to his feet.

"You think to get rid of *me?*" he snarled. "Laughable. It is because of *me* that our supply chains are stronger and more efficient than ever."

"And it is also because of you and that temper that our Fort Worth supply route has been torn to shreds," Silvadore countered. "And God knows what else your actions have caused. The U.S. authorities are all over our people, you idiot."

"I'm not a small child that you can bully any longer!" Estoban screamed, his neck veins bulging with rage.

Before Silvadore could register what was happening, his oldest child pulled out a silenced handgun, leveled it at his chest, and squeezed the trigger four times.

His mahogany chair tipped backward with him from the force of the impact, and Silvadore stared skyward, eyes huge, mouth opening and closing with shock and pain as his brain struggled to reconcile what had just happened to him.

"Your brothers will avenge me," Silvadore managed to wheeze in a small, weak voice as his life flowed freely from his wounds and pooled on the floor all around him.

"Once again, Papa, you're so short-sighted," Estoban chuckled, then clicked his tongue in disapproval. "I thought they might try, so, I already sent them on ahead of you."

Estoban's face morphed into a cruel smile as he lifted his weapon once more.

"Tell them I send my regards," Silvadore heard him mutter before a final shot pierced his forehead and sent him into the blackness.

Estoban didn't bother to hide his weapon as he strolled out of the lavish dining room. The butler approached and was summarily executed, as were the two most loyal of Silvadore's bodyguards that rushed toward him.

He found the other three members of his father's personal security detail wearing pale, pinched expressions and surrounded by his own security team just inside the front door.

"Well?" he barked.

"You have our loyalty, Patrón," the most senior of the survivors assured him, and Estoban smirked as the other two bobbed their heads rapidly in agreement.

"Good," he purred in satisfaction. "Come. We have much to plan."

His now twelve-member team piled into the two SUVs – except for the man that his father had personally charged with protecting him. At his request, that individual joined the new cartel leader in the limousine.

Once they'd left the property, Estoban flashed a feral smile at him.

"It's time to settle some scores, Javier," he announced suddenly. "Let's talk more about the agents you took pictures of the night Ramon was arrested. How is the research coming?"

Chapter Three

THE TOPICS of Estoban's conversation with Javier assembled in the eighth-floor conference room again on Tuesday morning.

"I've reached out to the city's traffic control division," Nathan revealed. "The goal is to get as much footage as we can of the day in question. I want to know if that truck was following Baker and Ben when they left the garage that day, and for how long."

He pointed to the overhead screen where the initial footage from the building's security cameras was cued and ready.

"We already know the truck that followed Wilford and Evans parked outside this building on that Saturday night. My gut tells me that when we watch the rest of this, that same truck will show up again on Sunday. Also, we know the route Ben and Baker took when they left here that Monday morning, thanks to the GPS device installed on the DEA's vehicle. So, it becomes a question of cross-checking every piece of video along that route that we can get our hands on."

Annie raised her hand.

"Yes?"

"But we'll only get video for so far along their journey, I would think," she pointed out. "Outside of city limits, chances drop dramatically of traffic lights having cameras."

"You're right," Nathan confirmed. "And at that point, we'd need to try to locate private sector security video along the route, if there is any. We'll get as much as we can and go from there. I am hoping that any footage we *do* get confirms whether it was only one vehicle on their tail, or more."

Lizzie chimed in with, "Did the lab get any data on that license plate?"

"Yep. According to the Texas Department of Motor Vehicles, that plate is registered to a 2010 Chevy Malibu, so, obviously stolen," Nathan replied. "Go figure."

Mark Calloway leaned forward.

"Any point in wading through all that garage video to try to pinpoint when the plates were switched out?"

Nathan mulled over his suggestion.

"Anything's possible, I suppose. But there's no guarantee that the trade-out happened *at that garage*. It'd be a needle-in-a-haystack search."

While the team contemplated the odds, Hank Myers worked his way through Albuquerque's morning rush hour.

He'd slept in a bit later than he had planned to and was scrambling to make up the time – not an easy feat when navigating congested roads in an unfamiliar town with almost a million residents. But his persistence was finally rewarded, and he made his way onto I-40 East.

"Next stop, Amarillo," he murmured to himself after a perfunctory check of his dashboard's gas gauge. "And with a little luck, I'll be at Nathan's place by six."

Meanwhile, on a sprawling 4,000-acre horse ranch just northwest of Granbury, Texas, retired jockey Theresa McNamara eased her favorite mare Gracie into the paddock for some exercise, then let her mind drift as the gentle giant dutifully plodded along.

A bad fall three years earlier at the Kentucky Derby had brought an abrupt end to Theresa's quest to become a premier name in the thoroughbred racing community.

Once she'd sufficiently recovered from her injuries, she'd switched her focus, and had been hired on to help run the popular ranch's outreach program. Each summer hundreds of kids flocked to the ranch for the chance to learn how to ride.

And although the future she'd envisioned for herself turned out to be very different from her reality, Theresa had discovered that she loved working with children.

Still, she often thought back to the day her lifelong dreams had been upended.

I wonder what would have happened to my life if I hadn't been in that race, she wondered for the millionth time. *What if Samantha Kennard hadn't been caught in time and I'd still been hidden away somewhere? Back then I was furious with Agent Thomas at the thought of missing my chance.*

But then again, she mused, *I wouldn't have been injured, either...*

The mare's whinny broke Theresa's reverie, and she smiled as she patted Gracie's neck lovingly.

"Sorry, old girl," she crooned. "Memory lane."

She laughed as Gracie snorted and pawed the ground impatiently.

"Okay, okay, let's go," she murmured, and brought Gracie up to a trot.

By twelve-fifteen p.m. Nathan and his team had reviewed the Saturday night video, plotted out the transport route, and the first round of traffic cam videos had arrived for review.

It was as Nathan had suspected.

The same black truck they'd seen in Saturday night's footage reappeared at around five a.m., its owner seemingly content to park on the FBI's doorstep, then watch and wait. The truck remained in place until late Sunday evening, when it drove away.

It showed up again at about six a.m. on Monday morning, and once more parked in a position where its occupant could watch both the front doors of the building and the exit of the parking garage.

When the team viewed the Monday morning footage, they could clearly see both Ben and Baker's faces in the front seat of the unmarked sedan as it left the sanctuary of the underground garage.

Nathan instinctively glanced Annie's direction and winced when he noticed her gaze fixed on Ben and her eyes misting over.

He turned his own gaze back to the wall screen and watched as within fifteen seconds the black truck sprang to life and pulled quickly away from the curb to follow.

"Here's a thought," Lizzie said aloud, causing Nathan to pause the video. "Maybe Ramon himself was marked somehow."

"What do you mean?" Annie asked after she'd swiped a hand across her eyes and cleared her throat.

"Well, he had a tail, right? But once Wilford and Evans drove him into that private garage, his tail would have lost visual contact."

"Yes, and?"

Lizzie rested her arms on the table.

"How would someone who doesn't have eyes on the target know when the target was being moved?"

"We're not even certain that he *knew* Ramon was on the move," Nathan reminded them all. "For all we know, this was a wait-and-see game. And not a very good one – I noticed no other vehicles coming around repeatedly, and we all know that on a stakeout, you don't just call it a night and go home and not leave anyone onsite. It's around the clock surveillance. But from what we've seen so far, it seems clear that the driver of that truck was working alone – at least at that point. I think he just got lucky."

"But," he continued, "to answer Lizzie's question, there are two things I can think of off the top of my head. If Ramon's tail was tipped off that they were on the move, then either Ramon had a tracker planted somewhere on his person that he wasn't aware of..."

"Or the DEA has a mole," Lizzie finished for him, and he nodded.

"Exactly. Which is more feasible?"

"I don't know about all of you, but I personally hope to God it was a tracker," Mark commented, brows furrowed. "The idea of our upstairs neighbors having a rat in their midst while we're going up against a drug cartel makes me anxious."

Nathan sighed.

"Me too, Mark. Me too. And, we know from what they pulled with Agent Jones that they've used trackers successfully before. So, let's at least rule the tracker piece of this theory in or out. Annie, please go to the lab," he directed, "and ask them to thoroughly examine the clothes Ramon was wearing when he died. They should still be in evidence."

"On it. Be right back."

Once Annie had left the room, Nathan looked over to his left at Lizzie.

"She's staying at your place for a while?"

"Yes."

"Keep an eye on her, please," he murmured. "We've barely scratched the surface of all this, and I have a feeling things are going to get rough. For all of us, but especially Annie."

As Annie visited the lab team, Hank drove past the eastern city limits sign for Amarillo, Texas.

Between a rumbling stomach and a plummeting gas gauge, his planned stop was quickly confirmed, and he exited the highway in search of both kinds of fuel. He opted for a burger, then filled his gas tank again before resuming his trip.

At the Cortinas compound in Reynosa, Mexico, Javier packed two bags, then headed to the ten-car garage where Estoban housed some choice rides. After some deliberation, he opted for the gun-metal gray Land Rover Defender.

He grabbed the corresponding keys from the numbered sets hanging on the wall, placed his bag in the front passenger seat, climbed behind the wheel, and pulled the vehicle around to the front steps where his boss awaited him.

A few last-minute instructions were issued before Estoban nodded once in satisfaction, then stepped back.

He could feel Estoban watching him as he smoothly steered the armored SUV down the long, winding driveway to the outer gate.

A handful of seconds to wait as the thick, heavy gate slid along its reinforced track to allow him to exit, and it was done.

Within an hour, he'd been waved through by one of the border guards and was heading north on TX-115 toward McAllen, Texas.

Javier's mission to mete out vengeance on the new cartel king's behalf was officially underway.

Annie resurfaced in the conference room a half-hour after she'd been sent to the lab.

"We struck gold," she confirmed with a determined look. "They found a tiny tracker sewn into the lining of Ramon's jacket."

"So that makes the possibility of a mole in the DEA much less likely, right?" Mark asked.

"Maybe – and maybe not," Nathan said carefully, his mind racing. "I'm not prepared to discount that completely just yet."

———

Hank Myers pulled into the Thomas household's driveway in Pantego, Texas at ten minutes past seven. He got out of his truck and stretched to try to unwind the mild stiffness that had settled into his muscles, then moved around to the passenger side to retrieve his duffel bag.

A grinning Nathan met him at the front door.

"I expected you an hour ago."

"Yeah, I know. Tell that to the construction crews," Hank retorted. "Does anyone ever get done working on highways around here?"

"Nope," came the sarcastic reply. "It's pretty much a constant thing all over the Dallas-Fort Worth area. Come on in. You hungry?"

"I could eat."

"You're in luck then. We made fajitas."

Hank followed Nathan into the kitchen.

"Bella, you remember Agent Myers," Nathan said as he made his way over to pour Hank a glass of iced tea.

"I do. Hello again, Agent Myers," she responded as she held out her hand in greeting.

"Please, it's just Hank," he replied and accepted the handshake. "And I appreciate your welcoming me into your home."

"It's no trouble at all. How about we get you settled into the guest room? I bet you'd like to set your bag down and have a meal."

"My thoughts exactly. After you, ma'am."

"Oh no you don't," Bella chided with a warm smile. "If you don't have to be 'agent', I don't have to be 'ma'am'. Please call me Bella."

Hank chuckled.

"Fair enough."

Bella led the way down the hall to the guest room as Nathan wrangled Charlie up and into his booster chair for the meal.

"I wonder what's bringing Hank into town," Annie said casually as she strained the pasta and Lizzie set the table.

"No idea. You never know with the DEA," Lizzie responded with a shrug.

"Maybe we'll get a chance to say hello," Annie mused, and Lizzie's eyebrow raised.

"What? He's a friend."

"Okay, okay," Lizzie put her hands up at Annie's stare. "I didn't know you two had gotten to know each other, that's all."

"He's called me every other day since Ben's funeral to check on me," Annie revealed.

"He did? That's sweet."

"I thought so. And I know he's had a rough go of it too, losing Cruz like he did," Annie mentioned. "We're in the same boat together."

Like Donny and I were, Lizzie thought but did not say.

After dinner, Hank and Nathan sequestered themselves in Nathan's home office with cups of fresh coffee.

"So, Hank, what brings you to Dallas this time? Working another case?"

"I'm relocating down here, actually."

"Really? When did that happen?" Nathan asked before he took a sip.

"When I got a gut full of that arrogant prick up in Seattle and I resigned from the DEA."

Hank paused, grinning, while Nathan recovered from choking on his coffee.

"You all right?"

"Dammit, Hank, you can't just drop news like that with no warning. What happened?"

"Well, the morning I went back to work, I got called into his office and told that I was being formally written up for insubordination. According to him, I was supposed to ask permission to come to Dallas and look for Cruz."

"I can just imagine how that went over," Nathan said with a dry tone and a wry smile.

"It went over just about like you think it did," Hank confirmed. "I told him precisely where he could shove both my badge and my service weapon before I slammed them both down on his desk and left."

"I can't say I blame you one bit. So, what's next for you?"

"I've made some calls, and there's an outfit down here in Pantego that I've got an interview lined up with the day after tomorrow," Hank revealed. "Private sector security."

"I don't suppose I could talk you into joining *my* team, could I?" Nathan countered.

"Are you serious?"

"If I wasn't, I wouldn't have mentioned it, Myers."

Hank tilted his head.

"Let's talk about that in a minute. First, get me up to speed on what's going on with Ben Tinsing's killer."

***

"Goodnight, guys," Theresa called out after another long but rewarding day of fielding questions from a group of eager middle-schoolers.

"We have another busload coming in the morning at nine," Kevin, the ranch foreman, reminded her.

"Yep, I'll be here. See you."

With that, she climbed into her truck and drove three minutes to the secluded half-acre she called home. Part of her ranch salary included housing; she'd been allotted a patch of land on which to set up her living quarters.

As she pulled up in front of her mobile home, she could hear her cat Mittens mewling loudly.

"Her food bowl must be empty," Theresa muttered as she locked her truck and hurried up the three wide, wooden steps to the front door.

When mewls turned to growls and hissing, two sounds she'd never heard her typically sweet-natured cat make before, Theresa paused and frowned in confusion.

"Hey Mittens," she called out as she unlocked the door and walked inside, then moved to her right to set her purse down on the coffee table.

"What are you..." was as far as Theresa got.

Sensing movement behind her and to her left, she turned her head and was met with a baseball bat to the center of her face that broke her nose, split her lip, and shattered her two front teeth.

The first impact had her seeing stars and knocked her off balance. Panicked, she slumped to the floor in a daze, trying her best to protect herself by curling into a ball.

It was no use. With every swing, her assailant's aim was true, and Theresa's battered body endured more direct hits from her attacker. Her ruined face was followed by a ruptured kidney, a fractured femur, three broken ribs and a punctured lung.

Just before the pain flung her headlong into unconsciousness, she managed to slur, "*Why?*" through bloodied lips and broken teeth.

But the only answer was another barrage of damaging blows.

As her beloved pet Mittens looked on, still snarling from her hiding place beside the overstuffed recliner in the corner, Theresa McNamara ceased to exist.

Her gloved killer casually dropped the bat next to the body, then leaned down to place a small, sealed envelope strategically in Theresa's purse before standing upright again to stroll out the open front door and disappear into the gathering dusk.

Three-hundred-twenty-five miles to the southwest, Javier activated the gadget that enabled him to scramble any security camera he wanted for as long as he pleased and went to work.

He moved quickly and quietly, and his task was accomplished in under three minutes. Whistling to himself, he strolled back over to the Land Rover, got in, turned off the jammer, and drove away.

Shame I won't be here to see this one in person, he thought to himself. *Oh, well.*

He drove north for another two hours before he opted to check into a Motel 6 in Huntsville for the night.

Chapter Four

THE FOLLOWING morning Javier was up with the sun. He started the single-serve coffeepot, then booted up his laptop.

"Lots to do," he murmured to himself as he navigated to the folder on the laptop that contained all the pictures he'd taken the night Ramon was apprehended.

By the time his coffee was ready, he had already formed a plan to deal with the first hands-on target on his list – DEA Agent Jacob Wilford.

Just need some light reconnaissance first for confirmation.

Smiling, he poured himself a mug, then padded to the shower. He got through his morning routine, dressed, packed, and was driving north within the hour.

In Pantego, Nathan and Hank met up in the kitchen for some coffee of their own.

"Mind if I hitch a ride with you?" Hank asked. "I'd like to help track down Ben's killer. Even as an unpaid consultant."

"I will not say no to another set of hands working on this. And you *will* be compensated. Come on, let's get to the office and read in my director."

He stepped around Hank to scoop Charlie up in a bear hug.

"Love you, buddy. Have a great day at daycare, okay?"

"Kay, bye Daddy!" Charlie replied with a mischievous grin before returning to his mother's side.

Nathan kissed Bella, then motioned to Hank.

As they settled into Nathan's car for the commute to the Dallas office, Hank sighed.

"Bella and Charlie are awesome, man. I hope you know how lucky you are."

"Yes, I am lucky. And, yes, I know *exactly* how much."

Annie finished dressing and pulled on her shoes, then stood and left Lizzie and Donny's guest bedroom.

"Morning," she said to them both when she reached the kitchen.

"Morning," Donny replied with a grin. "Got breakfast bowls ready to assemble."

"Breakfast bowls?"

"Yeah. We cook tater tots, eggs, and sausage or bacon, then throw them in a bowl and add cheese. Everything's lined out on the counter. Go for it."

Pleased, Annie grabbed an empty bowl and added a scoopful of tater tots to the bottom, then threw in some scrambled eggs and two pieces of sausage.

"Here," Lizzie offered and handed her a spatula. "It helps if you break it up a bit."

"Gotcha," Annie replied, and used the utensil's leading edge to chop up her bowl's contents before she added in shredded cheddar cheese. Her bowl filled, she moved to the table and added a bit of salt and pepper before she stirred the contents to melt the cheese.

"This is genius," she announced once she'd swallowed her first bite.

"We cannot take credit for this," Donny confessed as he built his own breakfast bowl but added diced jalapenos to his before he used the spatula to chop it all.

"How so?"

"One of the many things Liz and I have in common is that we both enjoy trying new places to eat. There's this tiny little place here in town that opened last month that makes truly awesome breakfast burritos, and we noticed that they mixed the ingredients together before they wrapped them in the tortillas," he revealed.

"Seems simple, but we were surprised that it made a big difference. Each bite had a little bit of everything in it. But the first morning we tried it here at home we were out of tortillas, so we just left it in the bowls," Lizzie finished as she joined Annie at the table.

Annie smiled, but it was wistful.

"Yeah, normally with a burrito it's hit or miss if you're going to get a bite with just egg in it. That's the whole reason Ben wouldn't eat them."

She paused before adding softly, "He was very particular."

Lizzie and Donny exchanged a knowing look before Lizzie reached out to squeeze her hand in a silent show of support. Donny did his part by switching topics after a respectful pause.

"Before I forget, I've got appointments lined up from nine to four today, Liz. The last one's up in Plano, so, I will probably get caught up in rush hour traffic coming back."

"No worries, we'll order in. Annie and I will figure it out on the way home."

By the time he reached Waco, Texas, Javier had already decided that using Ramon Gutierrez's place in south Fort Worth as his command post was optimal. The tiny one-bedroom house had been vacant since he'd killed its former occupant.

Not that Ramon's landlord would have cared either way, even if he *had* known that his tenant was no longer among the living. A carefully worded letter and three months' worth of prepaid rent on Javier's part had ensured that the clueless property owner thought Ramon had a family emergency in Mexico and that Javier was simply house-sitting.

And if the owner does *decide to drop by for some reason, I'll just add him to my to-do list,* Javier decided. *I'm going to war. What's one more body?*

He checked the Land Rover's in-dash clock, then the gas gauge, before smiling to himself and continuing north on Interstate 35.

Annie and Lizzie parted ways when they stepped off the elevator at the office. Lizzie headed straight to her desk to get her computer booted up first, while Annie opted to move to the breakroom to make herself a cup of hot tea.

She'd just unwrapped her tea bag and lowered it into a cup of piping hot water to steep when the breakroom door opened behind her.

"Well, hello there," she heard someone say in a rich tenor, and her eyes widened as she turned around to see who had spoken to her.

"Hank! It's good to see you," Annie exclaimed as she closed the distance between them to hug him.

"It's good to see you, too," he replied as he wrapped his arms around her and squeezed before he turned her loose and stepped back.

"Nathan said you were coming to town," Annie told him.

"He did, huh?" Hank remarked with a twinkle in his eyes. "So much for surprising you, then."

"Well, I haven't heard from you in a couple of days. I thought you might be mad at me," Annie teased.

"Nope. Just a lot of moving pieces lately, *especially* the last couple of days. Not the least of which was getting down here as quickly as possible."

"You working another case down here?"

"I quit the DEA and *moved* down here, Annie."

Her mouth gaped open in surprise.

"*What?* When did that happen?"

"The quitting part happened a couple of weeks ago. The moving down here part? It ended last night. Now I just need to find a place to live."

She punched him in the arm.

"And you didn't tell me?"

"*Ow,*" he exclaimed, then chuckled as he rubbed the spot where she'd popped him. "Annie, you have enough stuff going on. I didn't want to add to it."

"We're friends, aren't we? And friends don't keep each other in the dark like that," she scolded as she gazed up into his blue eyes from her five-feet-six-inch point of view.

"No, they don't," he agreed softly, and she watched the humor shining in his eyes turn to warm affection.

"Okay, so, we need to have dinner together tonight so you can fill me in."

"Sounds like a plan. What time should I pick you up?"

"Can't we just leave from here this afternoon?"

"I came here with Nathan," he revealed.

"And I rode in with Lizzie this morning," she said with a sigh. "Okay, pick me up from Lizzie's at six-thirty? I mean, if we get to leave on time, that is. You never know when a case will come in."

"True. And if one does – I bet we can figure something out," he quipped. "Now, quit hogging the coffeemaker."

"I'm not even using it, you big oaf," she teased. "Hot tea's my thing."

"That's all right, tiny, I forgive you," he shot back with a grin and made her laugh.

Nathan poking his head in through the open door interrupted their banter.

"Good morning, Annie. Hank, meet me in the director's office in five minutes," he intoned. "And bring me some coffee, would ya?"

"Um, sure."

Hank snorted once Nathan left.

"Geez. Volunteer to help and now I'm his personal barista?" he mock-grumbled as he pulled another mug out of the overhead cabinet and poured out coffee for two.

Annie smothered her snicker with her hand as she removed the tea bag and added sugar to her cup.

"So, I'll see you later, I guess," she said as she turned to leave the breakroom.

"Count on it."

By eleven-thirty a.m., Kevin, the ranch foreman, was furious.

Repeated calls and texts to Theresa's cell phone had gone unanswered, and he'd had to abruptly shift his crew's assigned tasks around to ensure that the busload of inexperienced visitors was adequately monitored around the horses.

When the picnic lunch included in the visiting group's day trip got underway just before one o'clock, Kevin took advantage of the break to stomp over to his truck and head to Theresa's place at the far end of the ranch.

But his fury swiftly turned to confused concern when he pulled up in front of her trailer and saw the door standing wide open. As he exited the truck he could hear what sounded like a wild animal's raspy screeching coming from somewhere inside.

"What the...," Kevin muttered under his breath, and strode quickly up the three porch steps. He rapped on the open doorframe as his nose crinkled at a weird smell wafting to him from inside the mobile home.

"Theresa, you decent? I'm coming in," he hollered before he crossed the threshold.

The moment he entered, the strange smell intensified into a sickly-sweet metallic stench, and Kevin whipped his head to the right to look over into the living room.

What he saw had him covering his mouth and gagging as he quickly backpedaled out to Theresa's front yard, snatched up his cell phone from the holder at his waist, and dialed nine-one-one for emergency services.

Since the ranch property was located outside of any city limits, three Hood County Sheriff's deputies and an ambulance crew were dispatched to the location. Almost immediately after they arrived, the senior deputy reached out to dispatch and asked them to also send an animal control officer.

The animal control officer's involvement, while not typical for a murder scene, was necessary – because a grieving Mittens had become fiercely territorial, hissing, biting, and clawing at anyone who attempted to approach her owner.

Once the cat had been safely contained for transport to a vet's office, the paramedics rushed forward, but they quickly determined that the petite woman lying on the living room floor in a pool of her own blood was beyond their help.

The senior deputy on scene radioed back to dispatch with a second request – this time for the Justice of the Peace to come and officially pronounce death.

As they waited for additional resources to arrive, the senior deputy spoke at length with a visibly shaken Kevin outside, while the other two officers painstakingly photographed the death scene and surrounding environment.

Within ninety minutes of Kevin's phone call to authorities, the still not positively identified victim had been gently maneuvered into a body bag, placed on a gurney, and loaded into the ambulance for a trip to the closest medical examiner – Dr. Broder's office in Tarrant County.

After that, the collection of physical evidence, including finger-prints, the blood-and-gore-covered wooden baseball bat, and a woman's purse, began in earnest. These were all carefully bagged and catalogued before being placed in an oversized evidence box for their own trip to Tarrant County – straight to its renowned crime labora-tory, and to Trish Wallace, the lab director.

Meanwhile, the senior deputy accompanied Kevin back to the ranch's main facilities, where interviews of Theresa's other co-workers began right after the tour bus full of customers left the visitor parking area at three-thirty.

Jacob Wilford's car left the underground garage promptly at five p.m. for the commute back home – precisely as expected – and Javier was ready and waiting.

He grinned and put the Land Rover's transmission into drive to follow along at a safe distance.

Banker's hours, Wilford? Really? he chastised the agent in his head.

When the married father of two pulled into his driveway a half-hour later, Javier discreetly drove past, then turned left at the end of the block to work his way back out of the subdivision.

At five-ten, Hank stopped by Annie's desk.

"You about done?"

"I am," she confirmed. "We still on for six-thirty?"

"I don't think Nathan is ready to leave just yet. Can we make it seven?"

"Sure. You know how to get to Lizzie's?"

"I don't. What's the address?"

She gave it to him and watched as he programmed it into his phone.

"Okay, then. See you in a while," Hank said with a wink and a smile before he walked down the hall toward Nathan's office.

Annie grinned to herself as she logged off from her computer and picked up her purse. She glanced up to see Lizzie watching her with a pinched expression.

"What?"

"Well," Lizzie began, then hesitated.

"Lizzie, what is it?"

"Let's talk in the car, okay?"

"Um, sure," a confused Annie responded.

The elevator ride down to the garage was quiet and it wasn't until she eased her SUV out onto the street that Lizzie let out a long sigh.

"Listen. There's something about Hank Myers that you need to know."

"O...kay...".

"It's just.... he's a player, Annie, and I am worried that he's got ulterior motives where you're concerned. You don't need any more stuff to deal with right now."

"A player? Seriously? That's hilarious. That man has never even put a *toe* out of line. He's been nothing but respectful to and supportive of me through it all. Why would you even say that about him?"

"Because, the first few times I interacted with him, he was very full of himself – the whole 'God's gift' vibe – and came on super strong. Kept asking me out and acted like my saying yes was a forgone conclusion. To his credit, once he realized that I was dating Donny and that it was serious, he backed off. But still."

Annie's nose wrinkled in distaste.

"Really?"

"Yeah, really," Lizzie confirmed. "To be fair, all that happened, what? Eighteen months ago? Two years ago? I could be way off base about him these days. Maybe he's changed."

She glanced over at her younger co-worker and friend.

"But what if he hasn't? I just don't want to see you get hurt, Annie."

"And I appreciate that, Lizzie. I do. But I'm also a grown woman, and not as fragile as everyone thinks I am."

"I know. Just putting it out there. I wouldn't feel like I was being a good friend to you if I didn't give you a heads up at least."

"I'll take it under advisement," Annie said crisply. "By the way, I'm having dinner with him tonight. He's picking me up at seven. So, you and Donny can order in whatever."

The rest of the commute from Dallas to Pantego was tensely silent, and Annie headed for the shower the moment they arrived back at Lizzie's house.

———

By the time Hank walked up on to the porch and rang the doorbell at Lizzie's house, Annie's flare of temper at Lizzie's comments had mellowed – to a point.

She's just watching out for me, that's all. And I appreciate it, Annie told herself as she slipped on her shoes. *But that doesn't mean I'm not going to call Hank out on what she told me.*

"Oh, hey. Nice to see you again, Agent Myers. Come on in," she heard Donny say in a surprised tone, and she hurried down the hall to the living room.

"Hey, you. Ready to go?" she asked, a little too brightly.

"Sure," Hank replied.

"Let me grab my purse. I'll be right back," Annie assured her dinner companion, and moved swiftly back down the hall to do just that.

"Okay, so, you two have fun," Donny quipped, and Annie

noticed the confused look he shot her direction as he turned to go join his wife in the kitchen.

Hank watched him leave the room, then turned his focus back to Annie.

"So, what sounds good? Anywhere you want to go is fine by me."

She tilted her head and considered.

"Surprise me."

He held out his hand and she took it.

Hank escorted her out to the front porch, closing the front door behind them, before he walked her to the passenger side of his truck and opened her door for her.

In the kitchen, Lizzie heard the front door open, then part of the conversation before the front door closed again. She slanted her gaze toward Donny, who had just walked into the kitchen and was looking at her with a furrowed brow.

"Okay, what's going on?" he asked. "I get home and you and Annie are super tense around one another, and then the doorbell rings and I'm expecting it to be the guy bringing our dinner, and it's Agent Myers? I didn't even know he was back in town, much less that he knows where we live."

Lizzie started to explain but the doorbell ringing again interrupted. Donny turned and went back out into the living room to answer it.

Moments later, he returned with a triumphant grin, holding up a bag.

"Now that's more like it. So, let's unpack this stuff and fill our plates and have a seat, and while we eat I can explain everything. Sound good?" she suggested.

He nodded and placed the bag on the counter.

Nathan had just finished his own dinner when his cell phone rang.

"It's Trish Wallace," a surprised Nathan told Bella.

"Something happened with Joe?" she asked, her face morphing into a worried frown.

"One way to know," he replied with a shrug and answered.

"Good evening, Trish. How are you?"

"I'm good. Sorry to call so late, Nathan, but I've had some evidence come across my desk that you really need to see. Can you come down to the lab?"

"It must be important if you're still working after seven p.m."

Trish chuckled.

"I'd still be here tonight anyway – Joe's out of town at a seminar, and my second shift tech called in. But I wouldn't disturb *your* night if it wasn't important."

"I can be there in twenty minutes."

"Great. See you then."

He hung up the phone and looked at Bella.

"Duty calls, huh?" she guessed, and he flashed her an apologetic grin.

"Yeah. Sorry."

"Don't be. It's the job, and I knew that going in," she reassured him. "Be safe, okay?"

"Always," he confirmed before he kissed her, then grabbed his keys and headed out the door.

"Let me see if I have this right," Donny said after he'd taken a sip of iced tea. "You told Annie about your history with Hank in an effort to try to warn her."

"Yes."

"And did it occur to you that he might not be that guy anymore?"

"Well, I mean... the last time he *was* around, he was fine. One hundred percent professional."

"Yes, he was. I remember you telling me that," Donny said gently as he leaned over and took her hand.

"Here's my point, honey. Once upon a time, *I* was a player, too. Remember? I told you all about that part of my past when we were hiding out in that cabin in Kentucky."

"I remember."

"So, I know firsthand what it's like to look back and reevaluate your life and reinvent yourself because you don't like who you are. *If* he's still a player, and he hurts Annie, I will gladly help hold him still so that you can beat the crap out of him. But we need to consider that maybe, like me, he's changed and he's not the same guy you had to deal with in Seattle. Give him – and Annie – the benefit of the doubt. All right?"

She nodded.

"Besides, Annie's tough. Trust me, if he *is* still a player, she will chew him up and spit him out and not think twice."

"Yes she will," Lizzie agreed with a grin. "You know, when I was trying to talk to her she mentioned that she's not as fragile as everyone seems to think she is. But I've *never* viewed her or treated her as fragile. Not once. And neither has Nathan."

Lizzie's brow furrowed as she thought more about it.

"My question is, who made her think that?"

"No way to know for sure, Lizzie. And it's not really our place to try and figure it out, either," Donny reminded her. "Things are going to go as they're meant to, and sometimes we just need to stay out of it."

Chapter Five

"Hey, Trish," Nathan called out after he'd rapped on the lab door and then pushed it open.

"Hey, yourself. Been a while. How are Bella and Charlie?"

"Bella's great, pretty much back to normal after a lot of hard work and physical therapy. And Charlie. Man, that kid is growing so much every day. Did you know that his fourth birthday is coming up already?"

Trish smiled.

"Time moves so fast. You turn around twice and he'll be in high school."

She paused, and her face took on a pensive gaze.

"What's wrong, Trish?"

"You need to see why I called you down here," she replied, and reached over to pick up two evidence bags to show to him.

Nathan grabbed a set of surgical gloves from the open box Trish pointed to. Once he had them on, she passed him the first bag.

"That," she indicated, "is an envelope. One with no fingerprints or DNA on it anywhere."

She handed him the second evidence bag.

"And *that* is the letter that was in the envelope."

Nathan carefully eased each piece of evidence from their protective coverings. He scrutinized first the envelope, then the contents of the short letter.

When he was done, he raised his head, eyes wide, and stared at her for a long moment.

"Where did you find this?"

"In the inside pocket of a woman's purse in the middle of a murder scene in Hood County," Trish replied.

"Whose murder?"

"Positive identification is still pending. The woman was beaten badly enough that simply comparing her to her driver's license wasn't possible, according to Dr. Broder. He's in the process of capturing her fingerprints and taking dental impressions to try to figure it out that way."

"Interesting... so, whose purse was it?"

"According to the wallet's contents, a Theresa McNamara."

"Theresa McNamara... Theresa McNamara... why does that sound familiar?" Nathan muttered.

"I have the wallet here, if you'd like to see the license."

"Sure."

Trish removed the small plastic card from the wallet and handed it over.

"Get out," he mumbled, numb with shock. "I know her."

"Based on that letter, I thought you might," Trish responded. "But how?"

He handed the license back, pulled off his gloves, and scrubbed his hands over his face.

"She was one of the jurors in the Harold Kennard murder trial back in the late eighties," he answered. "And about three years ago, I had to put her into protective custody for a while until his daughter Samantha was caught."

"I know about that case. Joe told me about it. Harold's daughter was targeting everyone connected with her father's trial, right?"

"Yes," Nathan confirmed on a heavy exhale. "And she killed most of them before we caught her. In fact, only Theresa and Donny Atherton were left."

He stood abruptly.

"I need to go see Broder. Thanks for showing me this, Trish. Is it possible to get copies?"

"Once I'm done with all my testing, I will scan them in and email them to you."

"Thanks. Keep me posted if anything else turns up."

"Will do. And Nathan," she said gently.

"Yes?"

"I have a bad feeling about this. Please be careful. Watch your back."

"Absolutely," Nathan responded with a certainty that didn't quite run to his core.

Hank had opted for an Italian restaurant, and they'd been seated in a corner booth. They made small talk as they looked over the menu and once their server had brought their drinks and freshly baked bread and taken their orders, she retreated to give them privacy.

Although part of her really wanted to mention what Lizzie had shared with her, Annie purposely tabled that topic for another time and focused on the first round of questions she had.

"So," she began. "Quitting the DEA. That's a pretty big move, Hank. What happened there? And why didn't you tell me? We've talked several times since then if it happened a couple of weeks ago."

"I know," he admitted as he pulled off a chunk of bread and spread butter on it. "But when they reacted to Cruz's disappearance the way they did, I became... well... disillusioned is a good word for it. I realized that to them, we're just pawns on their chessboard, not flesh-and-blood people. And it just made me so *angry* to know that the best friend I've ever had was disposable in their eyes."

He paused, and she watched as he reined in the stormy swirl of emotions that darkened his eyes from sky blue to angry ocean blue.

"After that it was just a matter of time, really. The idiot up in Seattle just pushed my last button on the wrong day, that's all."

He gazed across the candlelit table at her.

"And I wasn't about to dump my frustrations on you," he continued. "You've got your own matched set of baggage that you're carrying around these days. Like I told you earlier, I didn't want to pile on."

"I wouldn't have minded," Annie said softly. "Not at all. We're going through a lot of the same stuff right now. Although I wouldn't wish this on anyone, I have to say, it's nice having someone to talk to who gets it."

"It is, isn't it? Not quite so... lonely."

The conversation lulled as their meals arrived.

"Agent Thomas. Nice to see you again. I presume you're here about the Hood County case," Dr. Broder proclaimed as he scrubbed his arms from the elbows down, then grabbed a towel and dried off.

"Yes. I just came from Trish Wallace's office, and figured the next logical step was to pay you a visit."

"Of course," the coroner remarked. "Let me get some fresh gloves on and we'll get started."

He handed a pair to Nathan, pulled on another pair, and walked Nathan over to the rows of cold storage lockers along the far wall.

"I had just started another autopsy when she came in, so, I haven't had a chance yet to dig very deep," Broder explained as he opened a door and slid a metal tray out between them. "But facial identification won't work in this case. My assistant already pulled fingerprints, and I'll be making a cast of her teeth later tonight."

He glanced up at Nathan.

"You ready?"

"As I can ever be for this part," Nathan muttered, then gestured to the coroner to pull back the sheet.

"*Wow*," he exclaimed as he gazed at the woman's battered, crushed face.

"I know," Broder said sadly. "And unfortunately, I have a feeling that was among the first blows she was dealt. I won't know for sure until I get her on the table and do my full examination."

Nathan nodded and took a step back as Broder lowered the sheet over the woman's face again.

"I should have more data for you sometime tomorrow," the doctor announced.

"You know where to reach me. I'd say it's been a pleasure, Dr. Broder, but..."

The coroner grinned. "I know. Me too. Believe me, I'd much rather hang out over beers than bodies."

"See you later, doc."

"So, what's next for you then?" Annie asked once their dinner plates were cleared away and dessert served.

"Well, as I mentioned, I relocated down here. Everything I own is in the back seat or under the tonneau cover of my truck. I'm staying at Nathan's until I can figure something out."

"That sounds familiar, although in my case, most of my belongings are in a storage unit," Annie responded wryly. "Being at Lizzie's is temporary. I know Grace would let me move back in over there if I asked, but I really want to find a space of my own."

"Man do I understand that feeling," Hank agreed. "Part of my decision on where I wind up will be based on how the job interview goes tomorrow."

"What interview?"

"There's a private sector security company," he explained. "A friend of mine works there and he loves it. The people, the culture, all of it. Said it feels like family. Then he mentioned that they're always looking to add to their team. He gave me a contact name and I made a phone call. Long story short, I meet with the owner tomorrow at two p.m."

"Cool? Where is it?"

"In Pantego. Not far from the subdivision Nathan and Bella live in, as a matter of fact."

He leaned forward.

"Just between you and me, Nathan asked if I'd be interested in joining *his* team, too. So that's another option - *if* I decide to stay in federal law enforcement."

"Really? What did you tell him?"

Someone standing at the edge of the table and clearing his throat disrupted their conversation, and Annie glanced up to see Ben Tinsing's best friend Brody glaring down at them.

"Kind of soon, don't you think, Annie?" he snarled. "I mean, Ben's only been dead a month."

His hateful stare moved from her to Hank and back again.

"Or did you two even bother to wait that long?"

Hank raised an eyebrow and looked at Annie, as if to say *would you like me to handle this?* but Annie waved him off as she jumped to her feet and proceeded to get in Brody's face.

"Excuse me?" she retorted, one hand on her hip and the other curled into a fist with forefinger extended to poke Brody hard in the chest. "Not that it is any of your business, but I am having a meal with my *friend*. I don't know who you think you are, but you are *way* out of line here, Brody."

It surprised Hank to see their uninvited guest's shoulders slump, as if any fight the man possessed had suddenly drained away.

"You're right, Annie, I'm sorry. It's none of my business what you do. I just... saw you two and the candlelight and I just... I'm sorry."

Brody's cheeks flushed with embarrassment, and he spun on his heel and quickly walked away.

"You okay?" Hank asked her once she'd retaken her seat, and she nodded.

"What was *that* about?"

"His name is Brody. He and Ben were best friends," Annie explained as she reached out a trembling hand to pick up her wineglass. "And evidently, seeing me trying my best to continue to live my life in the wake of Ben's death pisses him off."

"Well, you managed it beautifully," Hank told her, and she smiled.

"Thanks. And you know what else? Thanks for not just diving in and trying to handle it for me," she blurted out. "Because Ben wouldn't have hesitated to wade right in and 'protect the little woman'."

Hank motioned for her to go on, and she sighed.

"Here's the thing. I did love Ben, and in his way, I think he loved me. And when we first got together, things were good. But as we got closer, his being so overprotective all the time just... wore me out. After a while it was smothering. I felt like I couldn't even properly do my job as a federal agent without setting him off in some way, and I began to resent him for it."

She took a long drink of her wine.

"That's why we were living apart when he died. He pushed too far, and I needed time and space to think about our relationship, so, I moved out of the apartment. He was killed less than a week later."

"That's rough," Hank said softly. "The way I see it is, you're not just processing his death. It sounds like maybe because he died, you *also* feel guilty now that you set boundaries and stood up for yourself when he crossed them."

He reached across the table and took her hand.

"If you're feeling guilty about calling Ben out on his behavior, you shouldn't, Annie. You are a strong, self-sufficient woman, and whomever you choose to be with needs to not just respect that fact but *celebrate* it."

She blinked back tears.

"Thanks. I'll keep that in mind."

"Hey Nathan, what's up?" Lizzie said when she answered his call.

"I'm not sure yet," he confided. "But I just came from Trish's lab and from seeing Dr. Broder."

"The coroner? Why? What's going on?"

"Does the name Theresa McNamara ring a bell?"

Lizzie closed her eyes.

"My dad's case from 1987," she answered immediately. "She was a juror at Harold Kennard's trial. Only her and Donny came out unscathed when Samantha and Lenny started killing."

Beside her on the couch, Donny tensed up, then muted the television.

"Well, they're going to have to identify her through fingerprints and dental records, but I'm about ninety-nine percent sure that the body I just looked at in Broder's cold storage is Theresa McNamara."

"Holy hell. What happened?"

"She was beaten to death."

There was a long pause.

"Nathan, what else is going on that you haven't mentioned yet?"

"The killer left a note in her purse, Lizzie."

"A note? Okay. And?"

"It was addressed to me."

"*What?*"

"Teresa McNamara's murderer left a note at the crime scene that was addressed to me."

Alarmed, Lizzie rose to her feet.

"What did it say?"

She heard Nathan exhale heavily.

"Among other things, it said, *I look forward to seeing you soon. We have a lot of catching up to do.*"

"Holy shit, Nathan," Lizzie breathed.

"I know."

"Do we need to make arrangements to...?" she trailed off as she turned scared eyes toward Donny, the love of her life.

"I honestly don't know yet, Lizzie."

"Are you home?"

"Yes, just pulled into the drive."

"We're on our way over."

She hung up as Donny surged to his feet.

"Liz... what's happened?"

"I'll tell you on the way."

As she scooped up her car keys she fired off a text to Annie.

Going to Nathan's. Not sure when we'll be home.

Annie had just climbed up into Hank's passenger seat when her phone chimed. As Hank closed her door then walked around to get behind the wheel, she scanned the two-sentence text from Lizzie and frowned.

"What's wrong?" Hank asked when he glanced over and saw her expression.

"Lizzie and Donny both went to Nathan's house for some reason," she murmured. "And I don't have a key to get into their place."

"Well, how about I just take you back to Nathan's with me? I mean, that's where I'm staying, so, not like it's out of my way, right?"

"That will work. I can just catch a ride home with them from there."

Hank grinned and turned the ignition key.

"Well then, let's go see exactly what kind of party is happening without us, shall we?"

But the playful mood that Hank and Annie enjoyed all the way to Nathan's house evaporated quickly once Nathan brought them up to speed.

"So, let me make sure I have this right. Somebody that you protected *three years ago* is dead, and someone killed her sometime in the last twenty-four hours. *And,* whoever killed her left *you* a note at the scene," Hank summarized back to the group gathered in Nathan Thomas's home office.

"Yep," Nathan confirmed.

"That's bizarre. Maybe I could understand it if you and her had kept in touch, or if it was a current case."

"I know, I think it's strange too."

"And the only other person tied to that case from three years ago is Donny, right?" Hank continued.

"Actually, no, he isn't," Lizzie interjected. "Joe Wallace and I were both hip-deep in that case. I think we ought to read him in too, Nathan."

"Agreed. Earlier tonight Trish mentioned he's out of town at a seminar," Nathan revealed. "But I think we need to get him on the phone."

Lizzie nodded and dialed her father's old partner's number.

"Hey Joe," she said when he answered. "I'm at Nathan's and there's been a strange development that we think you need to know about."

She pressed the button to put the call on speaker, then set her phone down in the center of the desk.

When Nathan finished retelling what he knew, there was a long, low whistle that emanated from the speaker.

"Well now, you don't hear that every day. That's weird. Did we miss somebody in Samantha or Lenny Kennard's backgrounds that might have taken up the cause where they left off?"

"Not to my knowledge, we didn't," Nathan answered. "And of course, there's the *other* question – why wait three years? It just doesn't make any sense."

"Nope, that doesn't add up at all," Joe's voice agreed loudly from the table's center. "I'll be back in town by about noon tomorrow, and I can come to your office, if you like."

"Let's plan on that, then. Around two p.m.?"

"Works for me. Watch your backs, guys. See you tomorrow."

"You too, Joe. See you then."

Once Lizzie had disconnected the call, she looked over at Nathan.

"What's the next step?"

"Well, among other things, we need to dig back into the Samantha Kennard case. We must have missed something."

"What can we do to help?" Hank asked.

Nathan levelled his gaze at Hank and Annie, seated side-by-side across from him.

"Since Lizzie and I are the two most familiar with both Kennard cases, we'll go back through them with Joe. Can you two take point on continuing to work the video footage we've gotten in?"

"Yes," Annie said without hesitation, and Hank nodded his agreement.

Nathan swung his eyes to Lizzie's left to look at Donny.

"I can't make you hunker down and stay home," he stated, "but I think Lizzie would feel better if you did. Just until we figure out what's going on here. And quite frankly, I would feel better, too."

"Fortunately, I don't have any appointments scheduled for the next week that can't be done via videoconferencing, so, staying home isn't an issue," Donny replied, and squeezed Lizzie's hand. "This isn't my first rodeo, so I get it. Better safe than sorry."

"Glad to hear it," Nathan replied. "All right, then, see you all tomorrow."

"Nathan, I have a question," Lizzie asked, and he nodded.

"Won't the DEA throw a fit about one of their guys helping us on a purely FBI investigation?"

Nathan glanced over at Hank.

"You want to?"

"You're fine, go right ahead," Hank said with a smirk.

"Nope, they won't have an issue with it at all – because he quit working for them two weeks ago," Nathan revealed, and he and Hank flashed matching grins at her when Lizzie's jaw dropped open in surprise. "As of this morning, he's an independent consultant assisting our Dallas branch office until he decides what he'd like to do next."

After the impromptu meeting was over, Hank walked Annie out to Lizzie and Donny's car.

"You want to ride in together tomorrow? I can swing by and pick you up," he offered.

"Sure. Around six-fifteen, if that's okay," she countered. "I'd like to go in a little early and get started."

"Sounds good to me."

"Hey," she said as he started to turn back toward the house.

"Yes?"

"Thanks for dinner. And for listening."

"Anytime, tiny. Anytime."

Chapter Six

As he did every morning, DEA Agent Jacob Wilford rose at five a.m. sharp and slipped quietly out of bed so he would not disturb his wife. He crept stealthily into the bathroom, where he changed into his running gear before he left the bedroom.

And just as he had every morning for the last five years, he did some light stretching in the pre-dawn stillness of his home's front foyer.

Once he felt sufficiently loose, he opened his door, stepped out, locked it behind him, and pocketed the single silver key in a specially made pouch of the reflective safety vest that he had added to his outfit.

Jacob pressed a button on the side of his watch to activate a timer as he walked to the end of his driveway, and when the readout cleared to zero, he released the button and started his trek.

The seven-mile circuit that he had perfected over time was a nice mixture of flat and inclined, pavement and nature – a large chunk of his run took him through the public park adjacent to his subdivision.

He let his muscle memory take the lead and cleared his mind, focusing solely on his measured breathing and the soft *slap, slap* of rubber soles against the concrete as cleverly spaced streetlights winked at him from overhead.

When he reached the entrance to the park five minutes later, Jacob made the veering right to take the steeper of the two possible walking trails that the city had so thoughtfully included in the park's design. As he did, he traded the glowing lights above for more subdued illumination – the city had opted to place ground-level pathway lights along the route.

He jogged along at his usual brisk pace as the path he had chosen wound its way toward, then into, a small grove of trees.

It was just inside the tree grove that he stopped short for a moment, then rushed forward to look more closely at a large shape blocking the path.

The dimmer lighting made it hard to see clearly, but Jacob could tell that it was someone lying on their right side facing away from him – and that the person was injured in some manner, because he could hear soft moaning.

"Hey, are you okay? Can you tell me your name?" Jacob asked as he crouched down and put a hand on the person's shoulder to try to roll them onto their back.

His eyes bulged, his mouth agape, as the stranger rolling toward him shot their right hand forward, then up and across to sink a dagger deep into Jacob's throat in a single, fluid, lethal motion.

The killer's momentum pushed Jacob off balance, and he fell to his right, desperately trying to form sounds to call for help.

But the dagger had robbed him of speech, and he could only stare, terrified, at the stranger who now towered over him with a satisfied smirk and watched the life fade from his wide, scared eyes.

***

Javier reached down with a gloved hand and checked for a pulse on the side of Agent Wilford's neck that he had *not* ravaged with his blade. Finding none, he nodded, pulled his weapon free, and stood upright again.

He stepped off the path and into the bushes to get to the small backpack he had stashed there. He pulled off the outer layer of his surgical gloves, taking care to wrap each one around the blade before he removed his blood-spattered zip-up hoodie and wound it around the murder weapon, as well.

He stuffed the bundle into the oversized plastic storage bag he had brought along, peeled off his second layer of gloves, and tossed them into the large plastic bag too.

Javier sealed the bag and shoved it down into the backpack before he zipped it closed, slung it over his shoulders, and jogged back to the Land Rover he had left at the north end of the park.

He tossed his backpack onto the passenger seat, retrieved his burner phone from the glove compartment, and sent a short text.

Then he started the SUV and began his drive back to Ramon's house to plan out the optimal way to take down his next target.

Hank arrived to pick Annie up at six-ten, and Lizzie answered the door.

"Hey," she said.

"Good morning," he replied, then frowned.

"Everything all right?"

Lizzie's sharp expression juxtaposed the level, even tone in her voice when she answered, "Everything's fine. Annie will be right out."

"Cut the crap, Zimmerman. What's going on?"

She raised an eyebrow, then stepped out onto the porch with him and closed the front door behind her.

"Fine. You wanna know? Okay, here it is. I don't trust your intentions with Annie, *that's* what's going on."

It was Hank's turn to lift an eyebrow.

"My intentions?"

Lizzie scoffed and folded her arms over her chest.

"Did you suffer a head injury recently? Or do you honestly not remember how much of a skirt-chasing dog you are? She doesn't need any more drama in her life right now, Myers, so back off."

"Woah, woah, woah. You wait just a minute, Lizzie," he growled. "I...".

The front door opening stopped him mid-sentence.

"Hi," Annie said. "Um... everything good out here?"

"Yep, never better," Hank assured her. "You ready?"

Annie rolled her eyes and muttered, "I know I don't *look* stupid."

Hank and Lizzie both took a sudden interest in the wooden porch planks under their feet.

"Fine, whatever. Let's get going, Hank," Annie suggested, and scooted past them both to walk to his truck.

Lizzie never broke eye contact with him as she leaned in close enough to Hank to whisper, "You hurt her, and I will *end* you. Are we clear?" before she abruptly turned, went back inside, and closed the door.

"*Wow*," Hank muttered to himself as he pivoted and walked down the steps of the porch to join Annie.

Hank hadn't even started the truck yet when Annie asked, "So, on the porch. What was that all about?"

"The short version is, Lizzie has an opinion, she's dead wrong, and I am going to take great delight in proving it," Hank replied with a mischievous grin as he turned the key in the ignition and put the transmission into reverse.

"Now. Did you want to stop for coffee somewhere, or just go straight to the office?"

"There's a donut shop with a drive-through window not three

minutes from here. Donny said they have excellent coffee – and I can personally attest to the quality of their hot chocolate."

"I vote we do that, then."

"And I second the motion," Annie announced and smiled back. "You fly, I'll buy. Deal?"

"Agreed."

When they arrived at the donut shop, the smell of freshly made donuts and kolaches wafting out to them from the open window proved to be too much to resist, so Hank and Annie ordered a dozen of each for the office in addition to their beverages.

"And a half-dozen cronuts, please," Annie added, and the shop employee working the window smiled and nodded her understanding.

"Cronut? What's a cronut?" a confused Hank asked.

"Just one of the most awesome things ever. Trust me, you'll see," Annie replied with a sly smile.

Mere minutes later they left the drive-through lane with two insulated cups nestled into the truck's cupholders, and three boxes of deliciousness perched between them on the center console.

"So," Hank said as he steered the truck toward the on-ramp, "you gonna let me try one of those cronut things, or what?"

Annie grinned, opened the top box, and handed him one.

He was only one bite into the succulent deep-fried and lightly glazed croissant when he glanced over at her and asked, "Hey – we don't have to share these with the others, right?"

"Nope," she said, and laughed, and Hank felt something twitch in his soul.

By seven-thirty, two detectives, the coroner and his assistant, and two members of the Dallas County crime unit team stood next to a walking path near a body lying sprawled on its right side.

The ambulance crew dispatched had remained onsite only long

enough to determine that unfortunately, their services weren't needed after all, and they radioed in for the coroner before they left.

Another jogger had happened upon the victim at around six-thirty a.m. and called emergency services. That pale, solemn young man now stood off to one side giving his statement to the junior detective as the senior detective took notes of his initial impressions of the murder scene.

Meanwhile, the techs photographed, measured, collected, and catalogued. Their tasks complete, they moved out of the way so that the coroner's team could retrieve the victim for transport to the morgue.

Other than a nondescript silver key, the male victim had no possessions on his person, nothing that could readily identify him.

When the junior detective finished speaking to the jogger, he walked over to join his partner.

"No wallet or car keys," the senior detective informed him. "Only what looks like a generic house key, so, I'm thinking he must live nearby."

"Maybe his wallet was stolen."

"Why would a thief steal his wallet but leave his wedding band and that expensive watch behind?"

"Huh. Maybe we'll get lucky and get a quick hit on his prints," his younger partner murmured.

"Here's hoping."

In Reynosa, Mexico, a still bleary-eyed Estoban Cortinas skimmed the text message he'd received.

One down.

Excellent, he typed back, then leaned over to his nightstand to snort his first of several lines of coke.

It was a little past eleven when Nathan's desk phone rang.

"It's her, Nathan," Dr. Broder said as soon as Nathan answered.

"Fingerprints back already?"

"No, she had a steel rod and pins holding her right femur together, and two plates and even more pins that were fused into her pelvic bones. I ran the serial numbers etched on the rod and plates. They came back as having been implanted in Theresa McNamara by an orthopedic surgeon up in Louisville, Kentucky three years ago."

Nathan sighed heavily.

"I was afraid of that."

Nathan wandered out to the bullpen area once he'd finished his phone call, and immediately noticed that Hank had taken up station at the desk lined up diagonally from Annie's - the desk that Nathan still thought of as Ben's.

That just doesn't look right was his first thought.

With effort, he shook that off to update Hank, Annie, and Lizzie on what he'd just learned from the coroner.

"Broder just phoned. I was right. It's Theresa McNamara," he told them.

Lizzie frowned.

"That makes zero sense at all. Like you said last night; why wait three years to kill her?"

He ran a hand over his face.

"I have no clue. But when Joe gets here I think we ought to..."

He paused when he saw his boss closing their position.

"Agent Thomas, please reach out to your second shift team and have them come in early. We'll all be meeting in the conference room at twelve-thirty. I've just had some news relayed to me that we need to review as a unit," the director said briskly.

"Yes, sir."

The director turned on his heel and walked away.

"Wonder what that's about," Hank murmured.

"Whatever it is, it can't be good," Lizzie replied.

"I have a bad feeling that you're exactly right, Liz," Nathan observed. "I'm going to call Herb and Mark. Grace doesn't return until tomorrow, right?"

"Yep," Annie confirmed. "The cruise ship isn't scheduled to dock in Galveston until sometime tomorrow afternoon."

Mark Calloway and Herb Davis arrived within ten minutes of one another, and Nathan's team moved as a group to the conference room.

Nathan was surprised to see the DEA's Dallas branch director walk in alongside theirs. Nathan's boss closed the conference room door, moved to the head of the table, and spoke.

"What we're about to discuss doesn't leave this room for now," he intoned, and when each team member solemnly nodded, Nathan's boss motioned to the DEA's branch director to take the lead.

"We received two disturbing pieces of news today," their visitor began. "First, multiple reports coming out of Mexico indicate that Estoban Cortinas has forcibly seized control of the entire cartel. We're still working on verifying the intel, but what we're hearing is that he killed his father *and* both his remaining brothers sometime Monday night."

There was a heavy silence in the room for a moment as Nathan's group processed the revelation.

"And you're sharing this with us why, exactly?" Hank inquired.

"Because we *also* got word that Agent Jacob Wilford was murdered early this morning. I don't think that's a coincidence, since he was one of the people that was directly involved in Ramon Gutierrez's takedown."

"He was *murdered?*" Annie exclaimed, her face deathly pale. "What happened?"

"He was stabbed to death while out on his morning run. The detectives working the case are reviewing video footage from the park as we speak. But I don't believe it was a random act. I believe he was targeted *specifically* due to his involvement in the joint task force's activities."

Nathan's eyebrows raised as he slid his glance toward Hank, then over to the FBI director, before returning his focus to the bearer of bad news.

"We had six agents onsite at the restaurant that night."

"Yes, I know. So, if I were you, Agent Thomas, I'd take steps to protect the five that remain - because I'm almost positive that he knows who they are, and it sure does sound like Estoban Cortinas' first order of business as the new king is retribution."

With that, their guest speaker turned to leave, but not before he addressed Hank directly.

"Myers, I'd like a word, please."

Hank's right eyebrow raised at the summons, but he shrugged, stood, and followed the man out and across the hall into a smaller conference room.

"I heard about what happened in Seattle," he was told the moment the DEA man closed the door behind them.

"News travels fast."

"It does in this line of work. For what it's worth, that guy has always been a jackass."

"Noted," Hank said, and folded his arms over his chest. "Why exactly are we talking about this?"

"Because you're an excellent agent, Myers, and I hate to see you leave just because your branch director was an idiot."

"There's way, *way* more to it than that. I believe you know that as well as I do."

"Yes, I do. But here's the thing – I need your help."

Hank scoffed.

"Give me one good reason why I should lift a finger to help the agency that got Cruz killed."

The DEA director leaned in close and whispered, and when he was finished Hank took a stunned step back from him.

"The hell you say. Really?"

"Really," came the solemn reply. "And you're the only one that has the skill set to solve it."

"Then that means…"

"That means it's not just the joint task force members at risk. So is everyone else stationed here."

"I cannot *believe* you kept this to yourself until now. You couldn't have said something when the task force was forming, so that they'd know what they might be getting into? It's not like you didn't have plenty of opportunities to mention this," Hank snarled, then began to pace.

"Opportunity, yes. Permission, no. You need to understand something, Myers. This was set into motion by the boys up in D.C. You and me? We just get to deal with the fallout from it."

"*Jesus.* I need to read Nathan in about this," Hank said heavily.

"*We* need to tell Agent Thomas - *and* his director," the DEA director corrected. "But only the bare minimum, and only to those two. No one else, Myers. I mean it. We need to keep as tight a lid on this as we can until we're sure."

"Let's do it now and get it over with," Hank growled. "I've got somewhere I need to be at two o'clock."

The DEA man tilted his head at that remark but simply said, "Then let's go back in."

They rejoined the others across the hall, and the visitor from the tenth floor stepped over to his FBI counterpart and murmured a few words.

"Nathan, I need you to stay a bit longer. Everyone else is free to leave," Nathan's boss announced, then watched as a puzzled Lizzie, Annie, Mark, and Herb filed out.

The quartet gathered in the bullpen after they'd been summarily dismissed.

"Did you see the look on Hank's face? Something else is going on, something that they're unwilling to share with everybody," Mark said, and frowned.

"I noticed that. But I *also* know that neither he nor Nathan will breathe one word about it if they're instructed not to," Lizzie chimed in. "So, the chances of the rest of us finding out what precisely is happening are slim to none."

"But why shut us out?" an irritated Mark asked. "From the sounds of it, everybody that was on the team that night is now in danger. Why would they withhold information from us that we could at least use to protect ourselves?"

"I honestly don't know. But they must have a good reason, Mark," Herb observed. "It must be something very delicate."

"No point in speculation, I guess," Annie announced, and put her hands up in a conciliatory gesture when Mark snorted in derision.

"Hey, I think we deserve to know the whole story, just like you do," Annie said calmly. "And for whatever reason that's not happening. But we all know our director would never intentionally put us in harm's way. We need to keep that in mind here."

Before Mark could retort, Lizzie interjected with, "And I don't think it's a matter of trusting us, either..."

Her brow furrowed as the seed of a theory planted itself in her mind.

"Wait, wait, wait. Think bigger for a minute. What would the DEA need to keep secret from everyone – *including* a sister agency?"

Mark's eyes widened just before he blurted out, "Oh, *man*."

"What?" Annie asked as she whipped her gaze over to him.

"That the threat we're dealing with is *internal* somehow," he shared. "I think maybe the theory we had about a mole on the tenth floor might have been right after all."

Motion and sound emanating from down the hall stopped their conversation in its tracks, and the four watched as a tense Hank Myers strode past the bullpen to the elevator and pressed the button to travel down to the garage.

"I'll be right back," Annie murmured, and walked away to follow him.

"Hey there," she said as she joined Hank on the elevator and casually pressed the button for the sixth floor.

"Where you headed?"

"I've got that interview at two, remember?"

"Oh yeah, that is today, isn't it?"

"Yep," Hank confirmed. "Where are you going?"

"Down to the lab," Annie lied. "Need to check in with them on some test results. Hey, want to have dinner tonight?"

"Can't. Sorry."

"Oh," she said, and tried her best to sound nonchalant. "Another night, then."

The elevator stopped at the sixth floor, and to keep up her pretense, she stepped out of the car.

"See you around, Hank."

He didn't respond, and the look he gave her was so intense it sent a chill down her spine.

The doors closing severed their eye contact, and Annie counted to fifty in her head before she pressed the button to return to the eighth floor.

"Well?" Lizzie asked her when Annie rejoined them in the bullpen.

Annie kept her voice soft and low as she answered,

"Whatever's happening, it's big, ya'll. Hank was super closed off. I'm talking way, *way* more than usual."

But any other comments were usurped by Nathan's appearance at Lizzie's side.

"Mark, Herb, since you two are here already, please work with Annie on reviewing that traffic footage. Come on, Liz, let's get the Kennard files prepped. Joe will be here in about an hour."

Chapter Seven

"It's nice to meet you, Mr. Myers," the receptionist at Cosantóirí LLC said when he arrived at ten minutes to two. "Right this way, please."

Hank followed her down the hall to an empty conference room.

"Mr. Jones will be right with you. Can I get you anything? Coffee?"

"I'm good, but thanks."

She softly shut the door on her way out, and Hank took a seat and settled in to wait. His phone pinged and he glanced at it.

Good luck! —Annie.

Hank sighed softly as he wrestled with his first instinct to respond to her, then thought better of it and turned off his phone instead.

Better for her this way, he rationalized. *Safer. At least until all this is over. I'll just have to beg forgiveness later.*

At two o'clock on the dot, Allen Jones, the founder and CEO of the private security firm, entered the room with his hand outstretched and broke Hank's reverie.

"Mr. Myers, welcome," he said with a warm smile, and Hank

stood and walked forward to shake his hand. "Would you like something to drink?"

"I'm fine, thanks. And please, call me Hank."

Allen grinned at him as they sat down.

"Very well. Let's talk about how you might fit into the Cosantóirí family."

The man leaned back in his chair and gazed at Hank.

"First and foremost, you come highly recommended by Jack Anders – and that's saying something, because he doesn't give praise easily."

———

"Nathan! How have you been?" Joe Wallace asked when the profiler met him in the building's lobby.

"It's been interesting lately, for sure," Nathan quipped as they walked side-by-side toward the elevator for the ride to the eighth floor.

Lizzie met them in the main conference room and greeted Joe with a warm hug.

"While the circumstances suck, it's good to see you again, Joe."

"Likewise. How's Donny?"

"He's good. How's Trish?"

"Well, she's still putting up with me. That woman deserves a gold star, I'm telling you."

"Oh, you," Lizzie said and chuckled as she swatted his arm.

They moved to join Nathan at the table, and the focus shifted immediately to the task at hand.

"So. Theresa McNamara," Joe announced as he set his laptop bag down in the chair next to him. "That's a name that quite frankly I thought I'd never hear again after we caught Samantha."

Nathan nodded.

"Me either."

"I know you gave me the highlights over the phone. I'm presuming we're going to dig back into that case?"

Nathan waved his hand toward the credenza along the east wall of the room where a row of cardboard file storage boxes had been placed.

"We are going to review both – Samantha's, *and* Harold's. Something in one of those cases motivated someone new to kill."

"I'll take point on lining it out," Lizzie offered as she walked over to the oversized dry erase board. "Because I don't know about the two of you, but even without my dad's notes I can still remember the name of everyone involved in Harold Kennard's trial."

In the smaller conference room across the hall, Mark, Herb, and Annie continued to trace the route that Agent Baker drove the day of the ambush.

"Okay, so, we have confirmation that the same black truck followed them down Akard Street, and then onto I-30 West," Annie summarized. "Did we get any of the footage in yet from Texas Department of Transportation?"

Mark typed furiously before he answered, "Not that I can find. But I can make a call and see what the holdup is."

A few minutes later he hung up the phone and grimaced.

"We should have it sometime tomorrow. Evidently whoever Nathan talked to previously didn't pass along the request."

"Great," Annie muttered. "That's just great."

She stood and marched across the hall.

"Nathan," Annie called out after she'd rapped on the closed door and then swung it open.

"Whatcha got?" he replied as he and Joe continued to unpack boxes and spread paperwork out across the long rectangular table.

"We've hit a snag. TxDOT *still* hasn't sent their footage. We won't get it until sometime tomorrow now."

Nathan sighed.

"Very well. How about you three join us in here? More hands might make this go faster."

"You got it. I'll be right back with Herb and Mark."

As he unpacked another file box, Joe Wallace noticed two thick manila folders with "L. Kennard" printed on each tab.

He glanced over at Lizzie, who was focused on writing out each juror's name from the original trial on the whiteboard. Satisfied that she wasn't paying him and Nathan any mind, he fired off a quick text.

Are the details about Lenny Kennard in these files?

Across the table from him, Nathan paused to read the message, and answered it.

Yes.

ALL *of them?* Joe persisted.

Yes, of course. Why? Nathan responded via text, then threw him a puzzled look.

Didn't we agree back then that it was best if we didn't tell Lizzie about who her boyfriend really was??? Joe fired back, then waited.

Nathan read the message, blanched, then typed quickly before he lifted his eyes back to Joe.

Crap. Yes, you're right. We did. You make sure that you're the one who reviews that piece, Joe. If she finds out about all that...

Roger that, Joe replied.

He rounded the table's edge to tuck those two folders away in his laptop bag. That accomplished, he stood upright again and glanced over toward the open doorway just in time to make eye contact with

Annie, who'd watched the entire silent exchange and whose brow furrowed in suspicion.

Fortunately, Mark and Herb appeared behind her moments later, and Joe breathed a secret sigh of relief that whatever comment she'd been about to make was diverted - because Nathan, unaware that he and Joe had even had an audience, looked over at his agents and smiled.

"Come on in and have a seat. Lots to wade through."

Two hours later they broke ranks, each tasked with reviewing facets of the two Kennard cases in hopes of finding something to help identify Theresa McNamara's killer.

Annie had volunteered to drill down into Theresa's life for signs of any conflict, just in case the note was a red herring designed to throw Nathan and the group off the trail of the real killer.

But it had piqued Annie's interest when Lizzie volunteered to comb back through Lenny's background and details and Nathan smoothly indicated that Joe would be taking on that puzzle piece instead.

As a matter of fact, he did it too *smoothly,* Annie thought to herself as she recalled the strange events she'd witnessed before they all sat down.

Almost like it was already arranged because he knew Lizzie might ask to take that part on herself?

She knew that in the Samantha Kennard case Lizzie had been a material witness, her official connection to the case one of kidnapping victim rather than active law enforcement officer.

But now, she's on the FBI side of things. So why wouldn't Nathan let her review whatever she liked? He's never purposely directed anything away from her before...

What is in those files that he does not want her to see?

And should I even say anything to her about it?

By the time she and Lizzie left the office at five-thirty, she'd come no closer at all to answering either question.

Once Annie got back to Lizzie's house she tried a second time to reach Hank, this time by calling since her text message earlier in the day had gone unanswered.

But instead of the phone ringing as she expected it would, it went straight to voicemail, so she left a message asking how the interview went, then hung up.

Not like him to ignore me. Not like him at all...

Dejected and unsure of herself, she plugged her phone into its charger on the nightstand, grabbed some clean underwear, a t-shirt, her pajama bottoms, and her robe and headed for a hot shower.

She spent ten minutes under the spray, letting the pulsing jets knead her shoulders as her mind wandered.

But every other thought seemed to involve either Hank's sudden shift in demeanor towards her or her gut feeling that Nathan was hiding something big from Lizzie, and she closed her eyes and fought the urge to scream at the top of her lungs in frustration.

Annie turned off the water, dried off, dressed, and made her way to the kitchen table for what she hoped would be distracting dinner conversation with Lizzie and Donny.

In the guest room at Nathan's house, Hank opened another browser tab on his laptop and continued drilling down to find the information he was looking for.

His interview with Allen Jones had gone well. So well, in fact, that he'd walked out of it with a job offer.

As a bonus, Allen had completely understood his need to take the next two weeks to tie up some loose ends before officially joining the private security company's roster.

Here's hoping it doesn't take me two whole weeks to catch up to

Javier, Hank thought grimly. *Every minute he's still out there, they're all still in danger.*

He kept working until just past ten o'clock, when he began to yawn. He saved and closed the file he'd been building, set his laptop aside, then reached over and turned his phone back on so that he could set his alarm.

Immediately, it pinged at him to indicate a new voicemail, and he pressed 'play' and closed his eyes when he heard Annie's voice.

Hey there, it's me. Sorry to bother you but I was just wondering how the interview went. I know you were excited about it. Um... anyway, yeah, that's all, I guess. Bye.

She thinks she's bothering me...

"If you only knew, tiny," he murmured. "If you only knew."

He wanted so badly to call her and talk to her, apologize for ignoring her...

Not until she's safe, dammit!

Hank heaved a deep sigh as he reluctantly deleted the message.

———

Over in Dallas's Deep Ellum district, Mark Calloway nursed his second beer and watched as the overcrowded dance floor teaming with patrons moved in time to the deep, pulsing bass of the music.

Being called in to work early had resulted in a benefit – he'd been able to leave at nine p.m. instead of his usual time of eleven. But he'd only managed to last an hour at home after work before restlessness had gotten the better of him.

I don't want to just cower in my apartment, he'd groused, then smiled as an idea came to him.

Yeah, that will work. Usually plenty of people there. Should be fine.

He'd showered, dressed, and headed to his favorite club for a couple of drinks. And as he'd hoped, the moment he stepped through the doorway he felt the tension melt away.

He'd just taken another small pull from the amber-colored bottle in his hand when a gorgeous redhead caught his eye and beckoned to him.

Mark grinned, set his beer down, and sauntered her direction.

Without a word, they began to dance, bodies pressed closely together as they slowly worked their way toward the center of the swaying, grinding throng.

He placed his hands on her hips to steady her and she flung her arms around his neck and moved even closer after they were jostled around by so many people occupying such a small space.

Mark had just leaned down to try to speak into her ear when he felt a sharp pain once, then again, that radiated upward through the left side of his back and took his breath away.

At the same time, his dance partner moved her arms lower, circling them around him just underneath his shoulders before sliding her hands down his back.

Her expression took on one of surprised confusion, and a puzzled and suddenly unsteady Mark looked down as she pulled her hands away from his body and held them out, palms up, between them.

They were blood-soaked.

The woman screamed loud and long when Mark lurched then collapsed at her feet and more blood from each knife wound he'd suffered rushed out to pool around and underneath him.

She tried to back away frantically, which drew the attention of those around her, and the crowd began to push and shove each other in their efforts to flee to safety. The wave of panic swelled into a tsunami when a handful of people were knocked to the floor and trampled on.

The lead bartender called police as the club's four bouncers waded in to try to restore order and render aid to the injured.

One of the bouncers finally managed to reach Mark Calloway's crumpled form lying on his side just left of center of the dance floor - and immediately keyed his mic.

"Get an ambulance here. *Now!*"

Hank had just drifted off to sleep when a series of forceful knocks startled him back to wakefulness.

"Hank," he heard Nathan call out, and he pulled back the covers, got up, and went to the bedroom door.

"Yes?"

"The director just called me. Mark Calloway's been attacked and they're rushing him into surgery."

Immediately Hank reached for his jeans and pulled them back on.

"Where are they taking him?" he asked Nathan as he flung the door open.

"Baylor Medical in Dallas," Nathan responded.

"Go," Hank urged. "I'll drive myself over. That way if one of us needs to leave for any reason the other is not stranded. You calling Lizzie and Annie?"

"That's next."

"Okay. I'll see you there."

As Nathan walked away, Hank closed the door and went over to the dresser to pull out a clean t-shirt and pair of jeans. He changed quickly, then grabbed his wallet, keys, phone, some socks, and his shoes.

A similar scene played out over at Lizzie's house. Annie woke to frantic knocking on the guest room door.

Annie opened the door enough to peek around the edge and blink sleep-filled eyes at Lizzie.

"We need to go. Mark's been hurt. Meet me in the living room in three," Lizzie informed her in a rapid-fire staccato, then turned and moved down the hallway and out of sight.

Oh, Jesus, was all Annie could think as she snatched up a pair of yoga pants and wiggled into them, put a bra and sweatshirt on, pulled on her socks and tennis shoes, and quickly brushed her hair up into a messy bun.

She rushed out into the living room with thirty seconds to spare just as Donny asked Lizzie, "Need me to go? I don't mind, babe."

"No, I'm sure he'll be fine," Lizzie said, and kissed him.

"Okay. You two be careful, all right?"

"Promise," Lizzie told him, then looked at Annie.

"You got your badge and sidearm?"

Annie retreated to her room long enough to grab both and stash them in her purse before she returned and nodded at Lizzie.

"I do now. Let's roll."

As Calloway's team members rallied to his side, his attacker sent another simple but powerful text to his boss in Mexico before he sat down to gather intel on his next target.

Two down.

Chapter Eight

THIRTY MINUTES LATER, a somber Nathan, Lizzie, Hank, and Annie sat and waited in a small room adjacent to the surgical suites at Baylor University Medical Center.

It didn't escape Lizzie's notice that Hank deliberately chose the seat furthest from Annie and completely ignored her.

Lizzie's eyes narrowed as she glared at him.

I don't care what's going on. No excuse for him to be an ass to her like this...

The sound of footsteps echoing across the tiles broke her train of thought, and along with the others she too looked up in anticipation – but it was their director, not a surgeon with an update as they'd hoped.

"Any word?" their boss asked as he joined them, taking the empty seat to Nathan's right.

"None so far," Nathan managed before he closed his eyes and rubbed them with his hands. "Nothing at all."

Another set of footsteps approaching diverted the group's attention. It was the lead detective assigned to the nightclub scene.

After introductions were made the newcomer said, "We're

pulling footage from the nightclub now. Hopefully, we'll at least get a glimpse of whoever stabbed Agent Calloway. Any word on his condition?"

"None yet, he's still in surgery," Nathan replied.

Mere minutes later, a member of the hospital staff finally came out to talk to them – and gave them news that each of them had desperately hoped not to hear.

"I'm so sorry," the weary surgeon said without preamble. "Agent Calloway's injuries were just too much to overcome. We tried our best, but he's gone."

Hank flinched at Annie's gasp of shock before he rose to his feet.

"I'll meet you back at your house," he told Nathan in a deep growl, then looked at the detective.

"Let's go. I want to see that footage."

"As do I," the director chimed in and rose from his seat. "After you, gentlemen."

The rest of the team stared silently after them as Hank, the director, and the detective walked out of the room. When the door closed again, Nathan turned to look at Annie.

"I think you need to activate your bug-out plan until this is over."

"I'm not leaving," she retorted as she wiped her eyes. "Not if I can help stop this guy."

"Don't you get it? He *followed* them, Annie. He knew exactly where Wilford would be at five-fifteen in the morning. He got to Calloway in the middle of a crowded nightclub, for Christ's sake. You're a target if you stay. And so is Grace."

"Grace," Annie breathed. "She needs to know about all this. Has anyone texted or called her yet?"

"I've tried to call but it wouldn't go through," Nathan answered, his voice and face loaded down with grief and weariness. "And this is not something I want to tell her in text messages."

"Try her again," Lizzie urged. "Maybe the cruise ship is close enough to port now that she'll have better connection."

As Nathan pulled out his phone to call Grace Womack, Annie

moved from her chair across the aisle to occupy the seat next to him, and the three waited, huddled together with bated breath as the call connected.

***

Grace answered her phone on the third ring.

"Hey, boss man," she said with a yawn. "You *do* know I'm scheduled off until Monday, right?"

"Grace," he replied, and the maelstrom of heaviness she heard in that single word made her entire body tense and alert, braced for the worst.

"What's wrong, Nathan?"

He sighed.

"Javier is what's wrong."

"Javier?"

Grace's brows crinkled up in confusion until she realized who he was talking about.

"Oh. That guy from the garage."

"Yeah."

"I don't understand. What about him?"

There was a long, heavy pause before she heard him say, "He's hunting us, Grace. He killed DEA Agent Wilford early this morning, and we just lost Mark."

Grace's eyes went wide as she sat bolt upright in bed and clutched her phone tightly like a lifeline.

"Mark... *Mark Calloway? Our* Mark? He's gone?"

"Yes."

"Oh, sweet baby Jesus," she murmured, tears beginning to cascade freely as she wrapped an arm around herself and rocked back and forth.

"Grace, I need you to do something for me," she heard Nathan say. "I need you to *not* come home. Activate your bug-out plan until I can catch this guy. Please. Promise me you will."

"But what about you guys?"

"I'm trying to talk some sense into Annie," Nathan told her. "And so far, it's not working very well. But Lizzie, Herb, and I weren't at the restaurant the night Ramon was seized, so for now, we can keep trying to capture Javier."

"But how did he even…"

"He was there, Grace. He tailed Ramon, and he watched the whole thing when you guys got Ramon back outside."

She gasped.

"Then Hank is in danger, too."

"I know, as does Hank."

He paused again.

"Now, can you go somewhere safe when you get off the boat in Galveston?"

"Yes," she answered immediately, her brain scrambling to launch her existing bug-out plan. "Yes. I have people that I trust in New Orleans that are on the job. I can head there. They'll help me however they can."

"Good. The moment you arrive, text me and let me know. And I will reach out as often as I can with updates, okay?"

"Okay. You tell Lizzie and Annie to watch their backsides. Hank too. I don't want any more calls like this one, Nathan."

"I know. Me either."

Grace Womack hung up the phone, set it down on the bed beside her, and gave in to the racking sobs brought forth by her friend and teammate's murder.

"Grace agreed. She's heading to New Orleans the moment she gets off the boat," Nathan revealed.

"Thank God," Annie blurted out, and dropped her head into her hands in relief.

"Now, let's talk about getting *you* to safety."

"I'm not leaving," Annie ground out, but Nathan slammed his hand down hard on the armrest separating them.

"Dammit. *No*, Annie. I am *not* losing another member of my team. Do you hear me? I'm *not*. You're leaving, and it's *not* a freaking request," he snarled.

"There's no point in arguing with me because I'm not budging on this," he continued as he crossed his arms over his chest and set his jaw when Annie started to protest. "I refuse to allow you to be another target. You're leaving even if it means I have to carry your ass onto a plane and strap you into the seat myself, and that's final."

"Fine. Then I'm going back to Tulsa," Annie snapped, after enough silence passed that made it obvious she wasn't going to win the battle.

"*Tonight*," Nathan stressed.

"Yes, *dad*," Annie retorted, her voice icy steel, and shoved up angrily from her chair.

"Come on, Lizzie," she growled. "I need a ride back to your place so I can pack and leave and be out of the way like a good little girl while the adults handle everything."

"Stop pouting like a child," Nathan snarled at her as he too stood up.

Annie's temper finally wrestled its way free of her grasp.

"How about this, Nathan," she began, both hands on her hips. "I'll stop acting like one when you stop treating me like one. I'm a freaking *federal agent*, just like you. I went through the academy just like you did, and by God, I pull my weight on this team. You're nervous that I'm in harm's way? Deal with it. It's part of my job. You had no issues whatsoever with putting me in a wig and a tour guide's uniform and letting some deranged psychopath with a rifle shoot at me. How is *this* any different?"

Lizzie's eyebrows ratcheted skyward as she took in Annie's vehemence and Nathan's brooding scowl.

"Okay, okay, both of you, calm down," Lizzie interjected as she stood and shoved her way between the equally mule-headed agents that stood nose-to-nose glaring at each other.

She blew out an exasperated breath.

"There's got to be a way to work through this that enables us to get this done with minimal risk to anybody. But right this second I really need both of you to calm down before you say things in anger that you cannot take back. Got me?"

Two grumbled answers of 'yes' reached Lizzie's ears in tandem.

"Good. Annie. Nathan and I cannot focus on catching this prick if we're worried about you getting killed. Nathan, I get that you're concerned for her safety – so am I. But it may take more than just me and you and Herb to find and stop Javier."

Nathan's throat worked violently as he got his emotions back under control, but when he spoke again his voice was still infused with a roughness that Annie and Lizzie hadn't heard since the day Ben died.

"The scene at Fort Richardson was different, Annie," he said, eyes downcast. "That situation was under our control. We had a much better grasp of his methods and his intentions, and we had contingencies prepared. But Javier's a wild card. A freaking ghost."

He lifted his head to look at them both, and Lizzie almost gasped at how much he'd seemed to age in the handful of minutes since the surgeon had relayed the news of Mark Calloway's death.

"He stabbed Mark in a crowd of people, Annie. How do we plan for that and keep you safe at the same time?"

"I don't know," she said softly. "I just know that we cannot break apart any further right now. The only way *any* of us will survive this is if we stick together."

"We're exhausted, and we're grieving. Let's all go home and try to get some rest, and we can continue to hash this out tomorrow, okay?" Lizzie suggested.

"You two go on ahead. I need to stay a while longer. Mark's sister and brother-in-law are already on their way here from Tyler,"

Nathan announced. "And I don't want them to be alone when they hear the news."

He paused, and his face showed raw emotion when he told them something that Mark Calloway never had.

"His sister is six months pregnant. Mark was about to be an uncle for the first time."

Hank was waiting in the living room when Nathan finally arrived back home.

"Anything on the club's security tapes?" he asked as he shut his front door and walked over to sit across from Hank.

"Yes and no."

Nathan raised an eyebrow.

"Yes and no? What the hell does that mean?"

"It means there was a disruption in the interior system's feed. We watched Agent Calloway make his way onto the dance floor with some woman, then the tape went fuzzy. Pretty sure Javier used a jammer to obscure what came next."

"Did it come back up?"

"Yeah, about four minutes later. But by then Calloway was down and the crowd was panicking. No clear shots of any one person besides him and the bouncer trying to help him."

Hank leaned forward to rest his elbows on his knees.

"But the exterior footage? That was more useful."

"Do tell."

"Saw a guy that sure looked like Javier walking outside and getting into a gray Land Rover. Couldn't get a clear look at the plate, but Dallas PD's lab is working on enhancing it."

"What was the timing?"

"Roughly two minutes after the interior footage turned to snow."

"And I suppose that Dallas PD will keep us posted?"

Hank's smile was feral.

"I asked them to rush it. I should get confirmation on the license plate any minute now."

"Good," Nathan said, and paused.

"I know that look," Hank muttered. "What's up?"

"Annie," Nathan told him with a grimace. "Even with knowing *exactly* what happened to Wilford and to Mark today, she won't leave."

"*What?*"

"You heard me."

"She *has* to, Nathan. It isn't safe for her to stick around here while Javier's loose."

"I get that, and I told her as much. She won't budge. Matter of fact, I thought we were going to come to blows in that waiting room over it."

"*Dammit,*" Hank grated through clenched teeth.

The two shared a long silence that was broken only by the phone at Hank's waist chirping. He plucked it from its holster and scanned the text he'd received.

"That's my signal. Guess I'd better get moving," he announced as he stood and walked down the hall to the guest bedroom.

***

A turbulent Annie Adams paced back and forth in the bedroom that she'd been staying in at Lizzie's house as an exhausted Lizzie watched her from the open doorway.

"This won't solve anything," Lizzie told her, and yawned. "Some sleep might, but pacing won't."

"I'm aware," Annie replied as she pivoted for yet another trip across the floor. "But we're under attack, and it's not going to stop, so we really need to watch each other's backs more than ever. But Hank's not only not answering my calls now, he's also straight up ignoring everybody but Nathan when we're in the same room? What is *that* about? Is he just gonna go guns blazing all by himself? It's not safe!"

"No idea," Lizzie said honestly. "And it worries me too."

"I mean... I just felt... I thought we were teammates. More than teammates. I thought we were friends," Annie murmured, her shoulders slumping in defeat. "And friends don't just start ignoring each other. Especially when some lunatic is after us. First Wilford and then Mark! And Hank's so closed off now I can't even... I'm worried about him, Lizzie. Really worried. If anything happened to him I..."

Lizzie stepped out of the doorway and into the room to grab both of Annie's hands.

"I'm sure you're still friends, Annie. And I think whatever's going on that we're in the dark about is the cause of Hank's sudden change. It sucks, but it is what it is, and I am sure it will all be resolved at some point. And once it is, you can ask him. But until then, we don't have any choice here. We need to focus on what we're working on, just like he does."

"Surely you've got *some* idea as to what's happening, Liz."

There was a long pause.

"I do, but nothing I'm prepared to speak to right now, Annie. Because it's just a hunch. Nothing I can prove."

Annie wrested her hands free to throw them up into the air in frustration.

"Why does it feel like our team is falling apart?" she ranted. "Javier's picking us off one by one, but instead of banding together right now like we should be, everyone's keeping freaking secrets, and I am sick to death of it."

She glared at Lizzie.

"Hank. Nathan. You. Even Joe."

"What do you mean, 'even Joe'?" a surprised Lizzie asked her.

Crap, Annie said to herself when she realized what she'd let slip out.

"Nothing, Lizzie. Never mind."

"Nuh-uh," Lizzie retorted. "You meant something by that. What was it, Annie?"

She folded her arms over her chest and stared until Annie's resolve crumbled.

"Ugh, fine. Earlier today when we all started digging into both Kennard cases, Joe stuffed some files into his laptop bag while you were writing stuff out on the board – *way before* Nathan handed out assignments for who was going to work on what."

Lizzie's nose crinkled in confusion.

"Really? From the case file boxes?"

"Yes," Annie confirmed. "It looked like he and Nathan were communicating back and forth via text, and Nathan got this 'oh crap' look on his face, and then Joe shoved some files down into his bag."

"While I was writing stuff down?"

"Yep."

"So *literally* behind my back," Lizzie muttered, her expression one of utter amazement. "But why?"

"I have no idea," Annie said, "but I'm betting it's something having to do with the one piece that you specifically volunteered to take – and that Nathan *specifically* handed off to Joe instead."

They locked gazes.

"Lenny Kennard," Lizzie whispered, and turned pale.

"What?" Annie asked, alarmed at Lizzie's sudden lack of color.

Lizzie closed her eyes as she answered.

"He... he was my boyfriend at the time, Annie. But I didn't know who he really was."

She opened her eyes again, and Annie winced at the hurt, haunted look that filled them.

"I knew him as Landon Kendal. It wasn't until Samantha Kennard was about to kill me that the truth came out."

"Oh," Annie responded. "*Wow*. Well, okay. I didn't know that. That makes sense now. Maybe they just wanted to spare you from having to relive any of that, then."

"But then why all the mystery? Why not just tell me, 'Hey Lizzie, we think it would be less painful for you if Joe takes this piece'? You know?"

Lizzie frowned and her tone and demeanor as she spoke morphed from hurt into a cold anger.

"I think that there is more to it than that. And trust me, the minute we get to work tomorrow, I *will* find out exactly what's going on. Thanks for telling me about this. See you in the morning, Annie."

Lizzie turned on her heel and headed down the short hallway to the master bedroom, leaving Annie standing dumbfounded and filled with guilt in the middle of the guest room.

What did I just do?

Hank Myers moved some of his belongings around so that his ready bag contained everything he needed. He zipped it closed, lifted it off the bed in Nathan and Bella's guest room, and carried it back out into the living room.

"I probably won't be able to stay in touch through this," he told Nathan, who nodded his understanding.

"Doesn't surprise me at all," the profiler confirmed. "Anything you need me to do on this end?"

"Look after Annie for me," Hank responded. "I know she's totally capable of taking care of herself, but I just...".

He paused and swallowed hard.

"Man, I hate that she won't do the smart thing and hide. And I hate that I can't even tell her what's really happening."

"I'm right there with you, man. I hate keeping secrets from my team like this. But we've got our orders. It has to be this way, at least for now."

Hank's phone sounded off again, and he skimmed the message.

"I'm forwarding this to you," he told Nathan, and did just that. "It's the license plate of the Land Rover."

End of Secrets

Twin lights illuminating the front window paused their conversation.

"My ride's here," Hank said solemnly. "See you around, hopefully."

Nathan held out his hand to shake Hank's.

"Here's hoping. Be safe - and happy hunting, my friend."

He watched as Hank grinned, picked up his bag, and walked out.

<hr>

After he closed and locked the front door again, Nathan turned off the living room lights and headed for the bedroom.

He got undressed and crawled into bed beside Bella, who softly asked, "Is Agent Calloway okay?"

The only two words he could force past his tightened throat were, "He's gone."

"Oh, baby. I'm so sorry," she whispered as she snuggled closer and wrapped her arms around him.

Chapter Nine

Lizzie purposely drove by herself over to the office early the following morning, her conversation with Annie repeating on a loop in her head that had rendered her unable to sleep much at all.

Donny had tried his best to talk her down off the ledge, but hadn't succeeded, and finally ceased his attempt by saying, "Well, just remember, Liz, Nathan must have a good reason."

With her husband's words ringing in her ears, she got off the elevator, marched straight down the hall to Nathan's office, and was dismayed to see that although his light was on and his suit jacket was draped over the back of his chair, her boss was nowhere in sight.

"One way or another, he and I *will* have a talk today," she muttered under her breath as she stalked her way to the coffeepot in the breakroom instead.

Annie exited the elevator an hour later and headed straight for her desk, glancing over at Lizzie as she walked.

"I guess you came in early to talk to him?" she asked and got a growl in response.

"He's in the director's office," Lizzie grumbled. "But he can't hide forever."

"Who can't hide forever?"

Both women turned to look at Nathan.

"We need to talk," Lizzie said, and fired a glare his way. "*Now.*"

Her tone caused both of Nathan's eyebrows to shoot skyward, but he swept his left arm forward in front of him in a 'go ahead' motion.

"After you, then."

She stood, stepped around her desk, and led the way to his office.

She settled into a visitor's chair and waited as Nathan calmly walked through the door, shut it, then moved to take his seat beside his desk.

"What would you like to talk about?"

"You're hiding something from me, and I want to know what it is and why you're trying to keep me from finding out about it."

Nathan sighed.

"I can't, Liz. Director's orders. I know you're smart enough to realize that it has something to do with the cartel, but..."

Lizzie leaned forward and narrowed her eyes.

"That is *not* what I'm talking about."

Pure confusion rolled across Nathan's face.

"Then what *are* you talking about?"

"Lenny Kennard."

His wince was a mere flash, a fraction of a second before he caught himself, but she still noticed it.

"Oh. That."

"Yeah," she huffed. "That. What the hell, Nathan?"

"First of all, back then you were not an official member of the investigative team, Lizzie. You were a kidnapping victim and material witness," he challenged.

"And I totally get that. It would have broken every single protocol to let a material witness see the case evidence gathered. But I am a member of your team now, Nathan, and I fail to understand why you'd reject my offer to review Lenny Kennard's file out of hand like you did – especially since he's dead and that case is closed. Unless you found something out about him *personally* that you do not want me to know."

She watched his face intently, and paled.

"You did. You dug into his life and uncovered something big, didn't you?"

Nathan remained silent until Lizzie's brow twisting forced him into speech.

"What?"

"I think... something Samantha said that day...".

Her voice trailed off as she closed her eyes and searched her memories.

"I remember her saying something about her brother keeping me in the dark even more than she thought," Lizzie revealed, opening her eyes again and staring at Nathan. "And I'm beginning to think that whatever it was you found out about him is what she was referring to."

"Lizzie, I..."

"Joe has those files, doesn't he?"

Nathan's shoulders slumped.

"He does."

"Then I guess I'm paying him a visit," she announced as she rose to her feet and headed toward the door.

"Lizzie."

The single word stopped her in her tracks, and when she turned around to face him she noticed the deep consternation that had settled across his features.

"Once you learn this, you can't undo it. You know that, right?"

"I appreciate your concern, but I'm willing to take my chances, Nathan."

Once she'd left, Nathan made a phone call.

"Joe," he said wearily, "Lizzie realizes something's up. She's on her way to you."

"What would you like me to do? You know just as well as I do that finding all that out could devastate her."

"I know. Let her see them, Joe."

"But Nathan…"

"Joe. I understand your concerns. I have them myself," Nathan confided on a heavy exhale. "But we both know she's tenacious. She doesn't let go of something once she's in investigative mode, so we really don't have much choice here. Let her see them."

"Then let's hope that she forgives us both from hiding it from her in the first place," Joe muttered. "Because she's going to be pissed off on top of hurt."

"I know. It is what it is, Joe. And hopefully, once she calms down again, she'll realize why we kept it a secret."

Lizzie stomped to her desk and grabbed her purse and keys.

"I'll be back later," she told Annie, then strode over to the elevator and jabbed the call button.

Mere minutes later, she fastened her seat belt, started her SUV, and left the parking garage.

She never noticed the driver of the gun-metal gray Land Rover that compared her face against his remaining pictures, then watched her drive away before he refocused on the building.

An hour later a deeply troubled Lizzie looked across the table, pale and wide-eyed, at Joe.

"*Eighty-four?*.... And the dates on some of these, Joe... he did some of these *after* we met... Is.... is all this true?" she stammered.

"The proof's right there, kiddo. They found it all on his computer. Rick even went and cross-checked every single international file he found against INTERPOL's databases. Everything tied together. All eighty-four kills, attributed to 'The Raven', aka Landon Kendal, aka Lenny Kennard. All closed cases now, thanks to what Rick found."

Her jaw dropped open even as shock gave way to unadulterated fury.

"Rick *Conner?* As in, my best friend's husband? He was in on this, too?"

"Come on now, Lizzie," Joe chided. "He was working as an official consultant for Nathan because he's got crazy good tech skills. It wasn't about you personally. It was about gathering as much evidence as possible."

"Until they decided to hide the fact that the man I was dating was a professional assassin," she snarled. "Then it *definitely* became about me personally."

"I know you're mad, Lizzie, but take a breath and just think for a minute. You know investigative protocols, so you know that even if Nathan wanted to, he wouldn't have been able to share that kind of detail with a witness. But even if he *had* somehow been cleared to tell you anything, you need to stop and ask yourself two questions."

"I'm listening," she muttered reluctantly.

"First, what good would have come of it, Lizzie? You had just been blindsided by finding out that Kennard wasn't who he seemed to be, and it shattered you, yet you still grieved for him."

Joe reached across the table and grabbed her hand.

"You want to be angry at somebody, be angry at *me,* kiddo. Rick and Nathan found all this stuff, they asked me my opinion about telling you anyway even though they didn't have clearance to, and I said no. Plain and simple. I couldn't spare you from Lenny Kennard's deceit or his death, but I had a chance to at least protect you from all *this*, and I took it," he told her gently.

She pulled her hand away and leaned back out of his reach.

"What's the second question?" she murmured, her calm, even tone a contradiction to her fiery expression.

He sighed but held her gaze when he answered.

"Would it have changed anything if you knew all this back then? The man still lied to you, he still hurt you, and he still died, Lizzie."

"Would you have told me if he had lived?" she fired back.

"Honestly? No. Not if I'd had a choice," Joe confessed reluctantly. "Like I said. You'd been through enough hell because of him and nothing good would have come of it. Telling you would have just added to your pain."

She started to protest but he continued.

"Hang on, kiddo. Let me finish. Here's the thing, Liz. If Lenny Kennard had survived, I wouldn't have *had* a choice. None of us would. Because everything he did would have come out eventually when the trials began – and all of it being made public would have caused a media frenzy that would have ruined your life. Just the fact that he killed anyone connected with his *father's* case made your life harder. Remember how those reporters swarmed you at the courthouse? So, yes, if he had lived, I would have warned you."

A long silence between them was finally broken when a seething Lizzie whispered, "I can't stay here right now."

She stood, picked up her purse, and fled the room.

"Wait. Lizzie, please wait," Joe called after her.

But it was too late. By the time he'd reached his receptionist's desk, Lizzie's SUV was already pulling away.

A half-hour later Lizzie parked, turned off the car's engine, and rested her head on the steering wheel while she gathered up the courage to get out.

Once her pulse was closer to normal, she climbed out of the car and made her way up the narrow path toward the tall oak tree that served as a directional marker.

As she approached her destination she seemed to step back in time, all the way back to the moment she'd last been here almost three years earlier.

Back then she'd been confused, conflicted. Raw. But this time, her feelings were infused with a laser-focused certainty.

She stood, silent and alone, a slight breeze rustling through the proud oak's leaves then dipping downward to playfully graze Lizzie's long brown hair as she studied the slab of polished granite that had been erected since her last visit.

It was plain, carefully bereft of any of the usual platitudes seen on headstones. No angels, flowers, religious symbols, or flowing scripts. Nothing emoting feelings of any kind.

Just two dates, and a name carved in basic block letters.

Lenny Kennard.

Lizzie stood and she stared until at last the dam broke wide open and the maelstrom spewed forth.

"You lied to me from the very beginning. About *everything*. Was there ever anything real about you at all? You reeled me in, made me fall for you, and the whole time you knew, you *knew*, that what you were would destroy me if I found out. How dare you, you... *bastard*. You utter and complete bastard," she snarled before she burst into tears.

She railed until she was spent, and as she wiped her face with her sleeve, one thought pushed its way front and center and took root in her soul with a vengeance.

I need Donny.

She abruptly turned on her heel and ran back to her car.

Donny had just finished his third videoconference with a client when he heard the front door open and close.

Confused, he glanced over at the clock.

It's barely lunchtime... Oh, God, please, please *don't tell me another agent was attacked...*

He stood and walked swiftly out into the living room - and stopped dead in his tracks when he saw his wife's pale, gaunt face, and her red-rimmed, puffy eyes.

Donny's stomach plummeted to his knees.

"Honey. What's wrong?"

"Can we go to the cabin in Vail for a few days? Please? I need to leave here for a while," Lizzie pleaded.

Donny closed the distance between them to take her in his arms.

"Let's go pack, and you can tell me what happened," he murmured against her hair as she clung to him and sobbed.

It was half past two when Annie rapped on Nathan's open doorway and asked, "Got a second?"

"Sure, come on in."

She entered, closed the door behind her, and took a seat.

"So, I got a text. Donny and Lizzie boarded a flight to Colorado, and they won't be back until Sunday night?" she asked him with a puzzled look.

"I'm aware. I've already spoken to Donny."

She frowned at his guarded expression.

"Nathan, what's going on?"

"Lizzie found out some things today that upset her."

"I kind of figured she might when I saw Joe stash those files yesterday."

"Ah," he said, and leaned back with a scowl. "So, *you're* the one that pointed that out to her and started this mess."

Annie flushed red.

"First of all, I didn't mean to. I was venting about everyone keeping secrets, and I slipped and mentioned Joe, and I tried to backtrack and just drop it, but you know how Lizzie gets. She glares until you talk. And I honestly didn't know my saying anything about it to anyone would cause so much damage," she replied, then bit her lip.

"And second, I had every intention of coming in here and warning you this morning, but she got to you first, and then she left mad, and I just..."

She took a deep breath.

"But then I figured that when she offered to review Lenny Kennard's files yesterday and you weren't exactly subtle when you ignored her and assigned them to Joe that even if I hadn't said one word about what I saw, she'd still have been suspicious."

"That doesn't matter. It was not your place, Annie. There was a reason why I didn't want her looking at those files!" he snapped.

A startled Annie jumped in her seat, and the stab of guilt he felt caused Nathan to purposely gentle his tone.

"But the damage is done now. Since Lizzie already knows, I might as well tell you, too, so you'll understand exactly why I am upset about it."

He filled her in, and she gasped.

"Oh, my God. No wonder you didn't want her to see those things," she murmured, her eyes filled with tears of genuine remorse. "I feel so bad, and I am so, so sorry, Nathan. I would've never said a word had I known."

"It's over and done," he replied. "Just – going forward, will you please come ask *me* about things like that, rather than speculating to another team member? If you had, neither of us would be worried sick about Lizzie right now."

He ran his hands through his hair and sighed.

"That's the problem with secrets. Some of them are too dangerous to reveal – and others are too dangerous to keep. And it's not always easy to tell the two apart."

"Like today, with Lizzie," Annie said quietly. "I know now that it would have been much better for her if certain details about Lenny Kennard's life had stayed a secret."

He nodded.

"Exactly."

There was a long pause until Nathan asked, "Was that all that was on your mind?"

"Well, since you asked, I'm tired of us keeping secrets from one another at all. Secrets are divisive and dangerous."

Nathan steepled his fingers and kept his face neutral as he stared back at her, but instead of taking the hint, Annie forged ahead.

"I'd bet dollars to donuts that whatever the DEA director told you and Hank that's so hush-hush, the rest of us could use to protect ourselves. Who knows, maybe Mark would still -."

He knew what she was about to say, and it burned him to his core that she was about to speak aloud the very same thought that had kept him awake all night long.

So, Nathan interrupted her, and his mask slipped as he fought for a second time to stay in control.

"You think I haven't asked myself the same thing a million times already? Don't go there, Annie," Nathan growled as his benign expression lapsed into rage, then hardened into indecipherable granite. "Just don't."

Annie gulped.

"Yes, sir. Sorry. It's just... I'm just..."

He watched her duck her head and fidget under his stare, her face filled with fear, frustration, and defeat, and his own struggle lessened a bit.

"I'm sorry, Annie. I'm taking what happened to Mark out on you, and that's not fair to you," he said in a calmer tone that had her raising her curious gaze to his again.

"I can't tell you what the DEA shared with me. Not yet, anyway. Believe me, I wish I could, because I agree with you. If my entire team had been read in, it is very plausible that Mark might still be here with us. But that's not the way it went down, and now the rest of us must live with the consequences."

He paused, then told her, "Like I've said before, I really think you'd be safer activating your bug-out plan, Annie. I cannot tell you more than that, even though I really do want to. I just need you to have faith in me and trust me when I say, not just as your boss but as your friend – you need to not be around here for a while."

A sudden revelation popped into Annie's head, and she gasped.

"I still don't think I need to, Nathan," she told him, then held her hand up so he would let her finish.

"Think about it. The night we captured Ramon I was under-cover, remember? I was 'Bianca', and because I was incapacitated, Hank had to carry me out of there and get me to the emergency room. To anyone watching, I'm a victim, nothing more."

"Possibly," Nathan conceded. "However, he's already killed two agents that were there. Javier strikes me as smart enough to figure out that you were there on purpose and involved in all this, Annie. Did he see you when you went to scope out the garage that day?"

"No idea," Annie replied, and her eyes went wide.

"What?"

"Well... he most likely remembered Ben the day he shot him. Ben showed up at that garage not ten minutes after I did. Ben said Javier changed his oil, and Ben wasn't wearing any sort of disguise. It stands to reason that Javier might have recognized Ben when he followed the transport team and ambushed them."

"I agree that he probably did realize the guy riding shotgun was the same guy whose truck he'd worked on. But let's go further and look at *all of it* from Javier's point of view for a moment. 'Bianca' and the oil change customer happen to be at the garage on the same day at the same time – and oil change guy is the very same man that Javier sees leaving this very building with Ramon and Agent Baker later that week?"

Nathan stood and began to pace.

"Now, if it were me, then I might look at that as just a fluke and dismiss it. But seeing that 'Bianca' is *also* in attendance when five agents arrest Ramon? To me, that would be much too coincidental to be just a coincidence. And my gut says that's the exact same way Javier will see it."

He stopped pacing and sat down in the visitor's chair next to her.

"So, we need to operate based on the assumption that he either already knows you're an agent, or is close to piecing it together, Annie. It's dangerous and foolish to presume otherwise because we know he does his homework - and he does it well. He knew *exactly* how to get to Mark and to Wilford. That's both impressive and frightening."

He leaned back in his chair.

"I also think he will be able to target more of us if we can't stop him soon," he said heavily. "Even those of us who weren't at the restaurant that night. My gut says it's not a question of *if* Lizzie and I might have to also duck and cover. Only *when*. Herb's already taken his wife and kids and headed to his in-law's place up in Tennessee."

Chapter Ten

ANNIE SWALLOWED HARD as the implications of what Nathan wasn't saying out loud hit her like a punch in the solar plexus.

Oh, my God... does Nathan think there's someone on our side feeding Javier information?

But she knew he couldn't confirm her suspicions, so she kept her voice level and even when she answered.

"I get it now, Nathan. Truly. And I'll pack up and head out to Mom and Dad's tonight."

He smiled for the first time since she'd walked into his office.

"Knowing that you'll be safer takes a huge weight off my shoulders, Annie. Thank you."

"Do you think it'd be smart to have someone ride back to Lizzie's house with me so I'm not alone there?"

"That's a very smart idea. I'll go with you, and you can drop me back off here on your way out of town. Will that work?"

"Do you know where Rick's bookstore is?"

"Yes. Why?"

"Because I don't, and I'm supposed to swing by there first. Rick and Faith have a spare key to Lizzie's place."

His cell phone rang, and he motioned to her to wait a moment as he answered it.

A few minutes later, he hung up and smiled again.

"That was Grace. The boat just docked. She said with a little luck she'll be on shore and headed to New Orleans in the next hour."

Their flight into Denver was routine, and Donny was supremely grateful, since his focus had been on Lizzie the moment he'd seen her distress.

He lifted their suitcase from the carousel, then slipped his free hand back into Lizzie's.

"Come on, babe. Rental counter's just over there," he told her, and indicated with his head off to their left.

She walked alongside him, still quiet.

After she'd calmed down, she'd thrown some items into their suitcase and then perched on the side of the bed and lapsed into silence. Donny knew that whatever had happened, she was still processing it all and that she would share when she was ready.

He'd left her side only long enough to book two seats on the one o'clock flight, then escorted her out to his truck.

All the way to the airport, through security, and during the entire flight Lizzie had kept to herself, staring idly out the plane's window.

But she'd never let go of his hand the entire time, either.

I've never seen her like this, Donny realized, even as he looked over at her while they waited for the reservation clerk to process documents and hand over the keys to a rental car. *And it worries me. Whatever happened this morning was huge.*

The rental transaction completed, he accepted the keys, and Donny and Lizzie boarded the shuttle to take them to the rental car lot to pick up the SUV he'd selected.

Down in Galveston, Grace patiently waited her turn to disembark, already planning mentally for her previously unscheduled but necessary drive to New Orleans.

She made her way down the gangway to dry land, one suitcase in each hand, and moved toward the booth for valet parking. While it wasn't a feature available to most cruise patrons, Grace's platinum membership in an exclusive travel club allowed her full access.

Grace sat one suitcase down long enough to pull her ticket stub from her purse and hand it to the young man working at the booth's counter.

"Sure thing, Ms. Womack," he said with a winning smile after he tapped some keys on his tablet. "We'll bring that right up for you."

He turned and handed the stub and a slender printout to another young man, who dutifully retrieved her keys and sprinted across the two drop-off and pickup lanes and into the parking garage.

She chatted calmly with the booth attendant for a few minutes while she waited. He'd just mentioned that he was pursuing a degree in marine biology at the local college when a massive, rollicking *boom* sounded from the parking garage, followed by another, even larger one.

The shockwave racing toward them caused the ground beneath Grace's feet to tremble, and she stumbled, clutching the counter, then whipped her head over her right shoulder toward the garage just in time to see a shaft of orange flame bloom and then disappear.

In a flash, she'd pulled out her cell phone and was dialing emergency services as she sprinted toward the garage, her suitcases forgotten.

"This is FBI Agent Grace Womack. We've just had some sort of explosion in the parking garage next to Pier Two."

Once they'd arrived at their cabin in Vail, Lizzie finally shared with Donny what had upset her so greatly, and her husband recoiled in shock.

"Did... did you just say *eighty-four?*"

"Yes," she confirmed as he gaped, open-mouthed. "He killed eighty-four people in a twelve-year period – and that's not even counting the people he killed that were connected to his father's case."

"He was a hired gun?" Donny summarized, and she nodded.

"Granted, his targets were not innocents by any stretch, so they probably got what they had coming to them, but the motive doesn't matter; it's still murder. Not only that, but some of those hits also happened *after* he and I met, Donny. He *knew* I was a cop, and he kept doing them anyway. That's what makes it hit so hard. It's terrifying to realize that if Samantha Kennard had not drugged and kidnapped me, I might have moved in with him, maybe even married him, and never known who and what he truly was."

She paused as she struggled to maintain her composure.

"To realize that someone that I trusted so much could have had me that clueless.... It just...".

"I totally get that, honey," he said gently as he reached over to take her hand.

"You feel the exact same way I felt when I realized that Sam wasn't at all what she seemed to be. I thought she was this great person, and all the while she was a cold-blooded killer. It was a real punch in the gut to find out that the only reason we even met is because she was going to kill me, but I guess she changed her mind at the last minute. Lucky me, right?"

He smiled hollowly as he squeezed her hand.

"Meanwhile, I bought her a ring – and I would have never suspected a thing had I not been looking for a pen that day. It's still frightening when I let myself stop and think about it. That one small, simple, random act is what saved me and helped stop her."

Silence lingered for a moment before either of them spoke again.

"It also hurts that Nathan and Joe and Rick knew all about this, and that they hid it from me."

"Baby, please don't take this the way it's going to sound, but – do you really blame them? Take a breath for just a second and really look at this thing. You're crushed right now at finding all this out about him, right?"

She nodded.

"They were trying to spare you from feeling *exactly* what you're feeling right now, Lizzie. It wasn't malicious. They knew, all too well, that knowing what he was would mess you up, so they opted not to tell you. And if this information is this damaging to you three years later, imagine what finding out back then, when everything was so fresh, would have done to you."

"I know. I know it doesn't make any sense to be angry about that," she confessed. "If I'm being honest, I'd have withheld this information too, had I been in their places. But I still feel a little bit betrayed."

"I get that – and I also know how you feel about secrets. You just need to keep their motivation in mind here. They're your friends, Lizzie. They were trying to protect you."

She leaned over to rest her head on his shoulder.

"I'm thankful for that," she whispered. "And for you. The single bit of good that came out of going through all that is that it led me to you."

"I feel the same. And I have an idea."

"Which is?"

"Let's leave *both* Kennards in the past where they belong. No more ghosts. Just the two of us, celebrating the fact that we made it through that nightmare and that we're here now, together, and happy. Let's enjoy a romantic weekend. What do you say?"

She tilted her face up towards his for a kiss.

"I say that sounds perfect."

He smiled down at her.

"Good. Want to go into town for steaks?"

"You bet."

It was just before five o'clock when Nathan walked out into the bullpen, grabbed the chair from the desk across from Annie's, and wheeled it over next to hers to sit down.

"There's been a development with Grace," he said solemnly.

Annie's heart leapt into her throat.

"*What?*" she asked, panic rising along with her pulse. "Is she...?"

"She's fine," Nathan assured Annie. "But according to the lead investigator onsite, preliminary indications are that someone planted a bomb in her car. My guess is Javier. Like I said, she's fine, but the poor kid who went to drive her car out of valet parking was killed instantly, as were two other valet attendants. Three others were hurt, one of them critically."

"But... how would he even know that she was in Galveston, Nathan? How is that even possible?"

"I don't know, Annie. I just don't know. There are only two good things about this. One, Grace is okay, and two, her car was only parked down there for five days, so we have a finite window of time to search. They're pulling security footage of the garage now. My gut says that they'll find an anomaly in the recording, like Hank found in the nightclub footage when Mark was attacked. That should help us."

"An anomaly?" Annie asked, deliberately avoiding any mention of Hank.

"Yeah," Nathan said. "Hank said there was about four minutes of nothing but static. We think Javier used a jammer to mess with the security cameras at the club, and I'd bet good money he did the exact same thing in that garage."

"So where is Grace right now?"

"At the Galveston police department giving a statement. She said when she's done they've offered to fly her to New Orleans by helicopter so that she gets there safely."

"Well, I know one thing for certain. If I was still on the fence about leaving, this would have sealed the deal," Annie told him. "I guess we need to get moving, huh?"

"Yes. But we're going to put you in a company car and leave yours right here in our basement garage where it's completely secured."

"You think he could…".

"Annie, if he was able to pick Grace's car out of a whole parking garage full of them down in Galveston, it's a safe bet to assume that he already knows what *you* drive, too."

"What about Hank? His truck is distinctive. Is he taking precautions, too?"

"He already has," Nathan told her nonchalantly.

Something in his response made Annie realize that what he'd just said was likely the only time she'd be getting any answers about Hank for the foreseeable future.

The thin tendril of fear that had wound its way around her heart in the surgical waiting room tightened its grip, and it took all her strength not to focus on her worry, but on her own plans for safety.

"So, how do we do this?"

"I've already requisitioned a car for you. We just need to go down to the motor pool supervisor's office, sign for it, and grab the keys."

Javier grinned and started the Land Rover's engine when a car carrying one of the men from his set of pictures appeared at the federal building's basement garage exit around five-ten.

"You'd think my taking out one of them already would make this guy *more* observant, not *less*. The DEA's training program must be seriously slipping," he chuckled under his breath as he left his parking spot to tag along behind DEA Agent Caleb Evans.

He drove deliberately, mindful of not only the space between him and his prey but also their surroundings, until at last the agent turned into the driveway of an apartment complex in north Arlington.

Javier followed suit, his movements unhurried, secretly elated that no perimeter security fencing existed.

Makes my job that much easier.

When the man he'd been tailing abruptly turned left to park in front of a three-story brick structure labeled "Building D, Units 101-304", Javier made it a point to drive past the man's position, so that he appeared to be just another resident who lived further back in the complex.

He pulled into a parking spot two buildings down, then backed out again and turned the Rover around to drive back the way he came.

He was pleased that his movements were perfectly timed – he drove past Building D again and glanced over to see Evans walking through the breezeway that halved the building and entering the far right-hand unit on the first floor.

From his research, Javier knew that the man would most likely hit the multi-family complex's onsite gym for an hour before preparing a meal and settling in to watch a hockey playoff game.

Not much to do now but wait, Javier decided as he exited the property and drove back toward the little bar and grill that he'd seen eight blocks to the east.

Roughly two hundred miles due west, Theresa McNamara's murderer observed from a distance as a certain couple came home from enjoying an early dinner and a movie.

The next intended target shuffled around to the passenger side of his truck to open the door for a short, curvy woman with a bouffant hairdo.

The older couple held hands as they walked toward the house together. Once they'd gone inside, the assassin started up the rental car's engine and drove away.

"He looked happy - and they do make a good couple," the killer murmured. "Too bad it's not for much longer. Enjoy it while you can, old man."

Javier entered the sparsely populated restaurant and seated himself at a high-top table in the bar section with a good view of the over-sized, wall-mounted television. The waitress brought him a beer and took his order before leaving him to his own devices.

While he waited for his dinner to arrive, he idly took in his surroundings. He glanced up at the TV and smiled like a Cheshire cat when he saw the breaking news banner pop up across the bottom of the screen. But the TV's volume wasn't quite loud enough to hear what was being said.

Javier immediately slipped his earbuds into place, then opened a web browser on his phone and navigated to the news station's website.

Within moments, he was gleefully watching a video clip of a young, svelte reporter whose bright red pantsuit stood out like a sore thumb against the drab gray brick of the multi-level structure behind her.

"The peace of a typically gorgeous April afternoon in Galveston, Texas was shattered today at Pier Two when what police suspect was a car bomb detonated in an adjacent parking garage. Three individuals were killed in the blast and another three were severely injured. While investigators are remaining tight-lipped regarding any evidence uncovered so far, an anonymous source revealed to this reporter that the vehicle in question belonged to a federal agent."

Javier raised his mug in a silent toast of triumph at the news before he paused the video just long enough to send another text message to his boss.

Three down.

Annie closed the trunk of the FBI-issued sedan and smiled at Nathan.

"Got everything you need?" he asked, and she nodded before he locked Lizzie's front door then walked down the front porch steps and over to the car to hand Annie the spare key.

"I packed enough for two weeks. Hopefully I won't have to stay away any longer than that."

"Yes, hopefully. Personally, I hope it doesn't even take that long," he confided. "But always plan for *more* time than you think you will need. That way you're not scrambling later."

They kept the conversation light as Annie drove them back over to the office. She entered the parking garage and stopped in front of the elevators.

"Thanks for going with me, Nathan. I appreciate it."

"Anytime. Do me a favor and text me when you get there," he answered. "And I promise, the moment it's safe to come back, I'll let you know."

Nathan watched Annie drive away before he headed over to his own car for the ride home to his wife and son.

As he fastened his seat belt, his phone pinged. Nathan scanned the brief text and smiled despite the situation.

Made it safely to the Big Easy – Grace.

"Good," he muttered. "Now we just have to catch this guy."

He fired off an acknowledgement text to Grace, then sent *FYI - Grace is safe, Annie's on the move* to Hank even though he had no idea if the former DEA agent would answer. While Nathan had been read in on the overall situation, neither he nor his director had received any specifics as to Hank's plans.

As a result, he was surprised when he went to set his phone down and it pinged in response almost immediately.

Roger that. Her car?

Company car, Nathan confirmed, then followed up by sending Hank a precise frequency setting for the long-range tracker that the motor pool mechanics had installed at his request.

———

Javier had planned to linger for a while after his meal, but the Friday night dinner rush at the restaurant had already started. He noticed that the tables all around him were rapidly filling up, so he paid cash for his dinner, then stood and left.

He checked his watch and grimaced as he strolled out to his Land Rover.

Great. Not even eight o'clock yet. Five hours to kill. Now what?

He glanced over to his right and inspiration struck.

Grinning, he started his vehicle and drove the block and a half to the coffee bar and internet café whose sign he'd spotted from the restaurant's lot.

Javier parked again, but this time he grabbed his laptop bag from the passenger seat.

This is perfect. I should be able to stay here for as long as I need to, he realized as he entered the place and was immediately shown to a table in the far corner that enabled him to sit with his back to the wall.

He ordered coffee, then unpacked and booted up his laptop.

Might as well do some work while I wait, he told himself, and navigated to the apartment complex website.

<hr>

Annie called her parents' house the moment she cleared the city limits of Dallas. It wasn't until the fourth ring that she remembered that they bowled in a league on Friday nights.

She sighed as she waited for the beep, then left a message letting them know she was on her way.

As she hung up the call, she fought back the sudden and intense urge to make another one – to Hank. Instead, she glanced at the illuminated dials on the unfamiliar dashboard to check the time.

Should be there around one-thirty, she confirmed to herself, then returned her full attention to the road ahead of her.

Chapter Eleven

It was one a.m., and he'd purposely changed his shirt so that he was dressed in black tactical clothing from head to toe.

Javier parked his Land Rover at the back of the complex. He added a few essentials to his person before he got out and pressed the button on his key fob to silently activate the door locks while he stepped up onto the curb and then onto the grass to muffle any sound.

He crept stealthily along, making sure to keep to the shadows as much as possible since a few residents seemed to be night owls – he could plainly see that more than one unit in the vicinity still had interior lights on.

One open stretch that contained playground equipment lay between him and his goal, but rather than scrambling straight across it to save time, he kept his wits about him. He reached down to extract the jammer posing as a cell phone in his belt clip and activated it to render any nearby security cameras useless.

Then he skirted the edge of the playground, blending into the tall, looming shadows cast down from the building to his north by the overhead streetlight.

At last, his back pressed against the exterior wall of Building D, apartment 104 – Caleb Evans' residence.

He closed his eyes for a moment to bring the schematics he'd seen into sharper focus. His search at the internet café had rewarded him with not only a detailed map of the entire property but also unit floorplans.

Once he'd mentally sifted through them to bring up Floorplan C, one that the website mentioned was an exclusive first floor offering, he smiled and opened his eyes again.

He pivoted, looked at the two windows next to his position, and compared them to the drawing in his head as he pulled on latex gloves.

Living room, and bedroom.

Javier glanced around to make sure no one was watching him, then risked shining his penlight on the living room window's frame for a few seconds to verify his suspicions.

Yep, wired to the alarm system.

But the tenant had not closed the blinds, and he was easily able to peek through them and verify that the area in front of the window was unobstructed. He then cast the thin but powerful beam up and across the room to locate the alarm pad, and his jaw dropped open to see a green light shining brightly, not the red one he expected.

Someone is either much too overconfident about their abilities, or an idiot. Either way, he'll find out soon enough what being lax about personal safety will get you.

Javier turned off and pocketed his penlight with a grin, then quietly worked the screen away from the window. The ridiculously simple lock fell to his talents in mere seconds, and he silently eased the window frame up, then reached inside and pulled on the long cord to raise the blinds out of his way before he climbed through the opening. Once inside, he turned and lowered the window back into place to maintain the illusion of normalcy in apartment 104.

Then Javier drew the weapon he'd tucked against the small of his back – his HK45 Compact Tactical – and swiftly screwed the suppressor he'd pulled from his pocket onto the barrel before mounting the compact night-vision scope.

With weapon ready, he crept his way across the room and down the narrow hall leading to the bedroom. The door was open, and as Javier looked through the scope he could easily see his soundly sleeping target lying face-up on the king-sized mattress.

He took three swift, silent strides forward to move to within a foot of the bed's edge and fired two shots – the first round to the head sealed Caleb Evans' fate, but Javier added the other into the upper left chest just to be certain. His mission accomplished, he used his penlight again to locate both expended .45 caliber cartridges and pocketed them before he turned and left the room.

Moments later, he'd returned the scope, silencer, and weapon to their original positions and raised the window again once he'd glanced outside to verify no one was watching.

He slipped through, closed the window behind him, and once again kept to the shadows as he retraced the route back past the playground. Only then did he turn off the scrambler and restore function to the complex's exterior security cameras.

When he reached the Land Rover and climbed inside, he placed his weapon in the glovebox, removed his gloves, fastened his seat belt, started the engine, and drove back out of the complex.

Annie pulled into her parents' driveway up in Tulsa a little past one-thirty. A blazing living room light reassured her that they'd gotten her message and were waiting up for her safe arrival.

She dutifully texted Nathan that she'd reached her destination before she got out of her car and retrieved her two suitcases from the trunk.

"Annie-bug," her dad called out from the porch. "Glad you made it all right, kiddo. Want help with your bags?"

"I've got it, Dad," she replied as she shut the trunk lid then grabbed one suitcase handle in each hand. "Hold the door for me?"

She maneuvered her way past her father and into the front foyer, and the moment she set her bags down he wrapped her up in a bear hug.

"Come on, girly. Let's sit at the table and you can fill us in on what's going on – starting with why you're driving a strange car. Did yours break down?"

"No. Mine is parked at work," she explained as she followed him into the kitchen where her mother waited.

"Hi, Mom," she said as she was engulfed in another firm hug.

"Come sit, honey. What's going on?" her mom asked the moment she turned Annie loose.

"Well, I will tell you. But you need to promise me that you won't freak out."

As she looked from her mom to her dad and back again, she noticed that both of her parents' faces became alarmed.

"I promise no such thing," her mother retorted, and pointed to a chair. "Spill it."

Annie sighed and took a seat. Her dad sat down at the head of the table to her left, and her mom occupied the chair to her right.

"I came back here to hide out for a while," she began.

"Why?"

"Because the team is under attack and my boss felt it would be safer for me here until the guy's caught."

A shrill "*What?*" accosted her from both sides.

"I might as well start at the beginning," she revealed, then swallowed hard and told them about Ramon Gutierrez and her role in the operation to arrest him, the garage raid, the murders of Jacob Wilford and Mark Calloway, and the attempt on Grace Womack's life.

When she finally finished speaking, she glanced at her father, who was staring at the table and whose face had taken on a pensive look.

"And this Javier person. Is he the same man that killed Ben?"

"We believe so, yes."

"You know, Annie-bug," he said slowly, "if he knew enough to get to your teammates like that, I'd bet he not only knows *exactly* what kind of car you drive, but all about your hometown, as well. That kind of information can be found pretty easily these days on the computer."

He lifted his eyes to meet hers.

"Provided he's even figured out that you're an agent too, that is. For all you know, he still thinks you're just some girl named Bianca that his co-worker took a shine to."

"That's what Nathan is hoping, but my boss is also a realist," Annie confessed. "He thinks it's just a matter of time before Javier figures out who I really am."

"Then maybe you ought to head for the lake house, honey," he said softly. "That thing's been in your momma's family for years. No traceability back to the Adams side at all. That might be your safest place to go until all this is over."

"Come with me, then," Annie urged. "If Javier digs past the Bianca cover enough to be able to follow me here, then you shouldn't stick around either. You two won't be safe, Daddy. He won't think twice about hurting you just to lure me out. He works for the Cortinas cartel. It's part of how they operate."

Her parents looked at her, then at one another, and when her mother nodded solemnly, her dad cleared his throat and answered Annie's plea.

"Okay, Annie-bug. We'll all go. Let's try to get a few hours of sleep. We'll pack up and head out at first light."

Javier waited until he was well clear of the area before he pulled into a parking lot just long enough to fire off another text message to Estoban Cortinas.

Four down.

That accomplished, a smug, satisfied Javier resumed his drive toward south Fort Worth and some well-earned sleep. As he drove, he narrowed his focus down to the last two people he'd photographed that night outside the restaurant.

One of them he already knew quite a bit about, and he'd already planned to wait and take out DEA Agent Hank Myers as his grand finale.

Looking forward to that, not gonna lie...

The other was the attractive blond woman that he'd heard Ramon refer to as Bianca. Javier had snapped a photo of Bianca as she'd walked into the restaurant, simply because she was gorgeous.

But he'd resumed taking pictures the moment that Myers showed up and then carried her limp body back outside.

The fact that a known DEA man had carried Ramon's date straight over to the very same car that Javier had since reduced to a ruined, charred heap down in Galveston was telling. He knew it was the same car – because Javier had taken pictures of more than just people the night Ramon went and got himself arrested.

His first assignment had been to take care of Ramon, and he'd done that in spades. Then a furious Estoban had ordered retribution on every federal agent involved – an order that directly contradicted Silvadore Cortinas' stern directive to lie low and let things cool down.

Having a clean shot of that license plate had enabled Javier to dig up plenty of information on one Grace Womack while he'd waited for some sort of consensus between the proud old man and his bull-headed son. He'd been inside Grace's apartment only long enough to photograph the cruise ticket held to her refrigerator with a magnet before old man Cortinas called him directly and issued new orders.

He'd put Estoban's missive on the back burner and immediately returned to Mexico to take up his new assignment - personally keeping Estoban safe from the Cortinas cartel's growing list of enemies.

Fat lot of good that did him, Javier acknowledged with a smirk as he recalled his conversation with the elder Cortinas. *The old man didn't realize until it was too late that the single biggest threat to Estoban is that white powder he shoves up his nose...*

He shrugged off the memory to return to the puzzle he needed to solve - the mystery woman named Bianca.

Myers was directly involved in grabbing Ramon. That much is certain, Javier thought to himself as he remembered the orders that Myers had barked to the others just loudly enough for Javier to overhear.

But who is Bianca? And what's her connection to Myers?

"I *will* find out," he murmured to himself as he pulled to the curb in front of Ramon's place and yawned.

After I get some sleep, that is.

By five o'clock that Saturday morning, Benji Patterson was up and preparing himself for another busy day out in Abilene, Texas. He did a double-take when he realized exactly what day it was.

Man, what a difference a year makes...

Writer Grant Forrester had approached Benji the year before and asked him for a guided tour of Fort Phantom Hill and Fort Griffin. At the time, neither man had any idea that the resulting article in *The Best of Texas!* magazine's April issue would be among the top read features of the magazine's entire history.

Overnight, phone calls and emails clamoring for Benji to take other visitors on guided tours began to flood into the magazine, as did questions about how the public could help preserve the rich heritage along the Texas Forts Trail.

The article had been read so many times – and resulted in so many donations - that the state's Historical Commission had offered Benji a speaker's fee for each tour he led at the two historical sites.

And after he had fully healed from his near-fatal gunshot wound, he had decided to accept their offer – but not before he had talked it over with Beverly, the woman he had been sweet on for years, and who had hardly left his side during his recovery.

Now, twelve months later, his days consisted of sharing his extensive knowledge of regional Texas history and enjoying life with Beverly.

He showered and dressed, then drove his truck up to the Waffle House, where Beverly's day had been underway since four a.m.

"What time are your tours today, honey?" Beverly asked him as she brought him his coffee.

"First one kicks off at eight," he answered. "You're still getting off work at two today, right?"

"Yes, Lord willing," she sighed. "Hopefully, the new guy will show up on time for the afternoon shift. But if he no-shows again, I will have to pull another double."

"I'm sure he'll be here," Benji said, and patted her hand.

"He'd better be," Beverly quipped. "Because I've already got plans with my sweetie this evening."

"Darn right you do," he exclaimed, and winked at her.

She leaned over and kissed him before she went to put in his usual order with the cook.

Gettin' paid to talk about what I love, and spending time with the woman I love. It just don't get no better than that, Benji thought to himself, and smiled as he sipped his coffee.

Up in Oklahoma, Annie and her parents filled three coolers with foodstuffs and other supplies they would need. Her father loaded them into the bed of his truck as Annie put her bags back into the trunk of her FBI-issued sedan.

"You sure you don't want to just ride with us?" her mom asked as she carried two suitcases of clothes out to her husband, and Annie shook her head.

"I'm sure. Call it a hunch, but I feel like we need to be ready to go different directions if the worst should happen," Annie said, a stubborn expression firmly etched on her face.

Her mom chuckled.

"You couldn't look any more like your dad right now if you tried," she told her daughter.

"I heard that," came the retort from behind them. "You two ready? We need to get moving. It's a three-hour ride."

The morning's guided tours at Fort Griffin had all been rescheduled for the afternoon due to a heavy thunderstorm that had rolled in from the west.

But fifty miles separated the two historical sites, and when he pulled up his phone's weather app Benji Patterson was pleased to see that the rogue rain showers were bypassing Fort Phantom Hill's location completely.

Might as well get that one done while I'm waiting, he thought to himself, and dialed a number.

When the out-of-town visitor answered, he explained the situation and asked if they could move up the scheduled tour time. His suggestion was met with enthusiasm.

"Yes, that will work well for me, too. Around ten?"

"Great. I'll meet you out there."

Benji hung up the phone, started his truck, and began the drive south and west to Fort Phantom Hill.

As Benji headed out to meet his client, a still yawning Javier booted up his laptop, then added more notes to the file folder dedicated to hunting down the mysterious Bianca.

The more he thought about it, the less he was convinced that

Bianca had nothing to do with the events that led to Ramon being hauled away.

But he didn't even know her full name, much less anything else that could prove what his gut was screaming to be the truth.

"Dammit," he seethed. "Should have interrogated one of them first. Evans probably would have sung like a canary."

Frustrated, he leaned back.

"I guess Grace's apartment is as good a place as any to keep digging," he said to himself, and shrugged. "Maybe I'll get lucky."

Benji pulled into the tiny roadside lot at Phantom Hill at nine-fifty and was pleased to see that his client was already there.

"Morning, I'm Benji," he said, and as he strode forward to shake hands, he noticed the bulky-looking bag.

"It's my camera equipment," came the explanation. "I'm hoping to get some really good shots."

"If you like history at all, you'll have some excellent chances," Benji answered. "Shall we get started?"

They walked side-by-side as Benji launched into the Phantom Hill story that he'd told time and time again. He pointed out various ruins and tried his best to bring the fort to life again for his companion.

Eventually, they reached the far end of the property where the remnants of the commissary still stood, and Benji began to describe the once-proud, two-story structure that was a marvel in its day.

"I'd like to get a picture of you in front of the stone wall, if that's all right," his visitor suggested, and he beamed.

"Sure, happy to."

He ambled over to position himself, squinting in the sunlight.

"Are you ready?"

"Go for it," Benji replied as he turned around to face his client.

But as he'd turned his back and walked, his companion had

reached into the camera bag and pulled out an altogether different tool with which to take shots in the rugged landscape.

The first bullet pierced Benji's upper left chest and flung him back, hard. He slammed against the six-foot-high stone wall as the second round tore another path through his body, followed quickly by two more.

He slumped, then slid down to the ground, his blood smeared against the old stone structure as some sort of macabre homage to one of the places he'd loved best.

His killer waited a few moments before closing the distance to confirm that he was dead, then tucked a small, sealed envelope into the front pocket of Benji's jeans.

With the mission completed, the revolver was repacked into the camera bag, and Benji's mysterious assailant walked away.

Annie followed her dad's truck through the gate and across the cattle guard, then parked her car, jumped out, and swung the gate shut again before securing the padlock back on the thick chain.

"Man, this brings back memories," she said to herself and gave her dad a thumbs-up sign and a huge grin before she got back behind the wheel.

Their 'lake house', as her dad called it, was a three-bedroom log cabin nestled on twenty acres northwest of Bee, Oklahoma. The acreage shared a border with the southern edge of the Tishomingo National Wildlife Refuge, a preserve cradling the northernmost section of Lake Texoma. The property's location meant that from the north, at least, the Adams would never have to worry about civilization ruining the view.

Annie had spent many carefree summers here with her family and had always felt a peaceful happiness each time she'd visited the cabin.

Let's hope this trip is no different.

She pulled her car to a stop next to her father's truck in front of the cabin and the trio began the process of unloading luggage and groceries.

Beverly was relieved when the new kid showed up on time, and she smiled as she removed her apron and clocked out at two-oh-two.

"See you guys tomorrow," she called out to the line cooks and to Amos, the owner.

The moment she got out to her car, she called Benji. The phone rang five times before going to voicemail, but since she knew he had tours booked all day she didn't think much of it.

"Hey, sweetie," she said after the beep sounded. "I'm off work and heading home. Just wanted to let you know. I'll see you around seven, okay? Love you."

Javier's plan to snoop around in Grace's two-bedroom Dallas apartment had nearly been thwarted by a nosy neighbor. Luckily, he'd managed to dress enough like a package deliveryman that the suspicious man was mollified and left him to his own devices. The moment he was sure the coast was clear he'd jammed the security cameras long enough to pick the lock and sneak into the unit.

He took his time, carefully combing through Grace Womack's day planner and her computer as well as rummaging around in various cabinets and drawers.

A small stack of mail on the kitchen countertop caught his eye, and he tilted his head in confusion as he noticed the temporary forwarding labels affixed to each envelope.

Annie Adams. Who's that?

He immediately went to the second bedroom to verify whether a roommate was in residence. But one glance at the empty closet confirmed Grace still lived alone.

Whoever this Annie person is, she's gonna be so pissed that I blew up the person collecting her mail for her, Javier thought to himself with a devilish grin before he resuming searching through the quiet space.

But after almost ninety minutes, he had found nothing at all that could help him find out more about Bianca.

It's a setback, not the end, Javier told himself as his mind raced. *I just need one thread to pull, that's all. Just one.*

As he mulled over his remaining options, Javier was suddenly broadsided by a novel idea.

He immediately opened a new browser window on Grace's computer and began to look for news coverage from the day he'd chased down and taken out Ramon and his handlers.

He clicked 'play', watched the video again, and grinned.

That's right. The driver lived. Looks like it's time to pay him a visit and see how well that left shoulder is healing up. I bet I can make him sing just fine.

Javier made sure to erase his search history before he scrambled the cameras again, then risked a peek out the door to make sure the coast was clear. Seeing no one around, he quickly exited the apartment, locking the door securely behind him, and strolled away. He waited until he was back in his Land Rover to turn off the signal jammer before he drove away.

Next step, track down one Patrick Baker.

Chapter Twelve

WHEN SHE HADN'T SEEN or heard back from Benji by five o'clock, Beverly called again and left another message. And she did so again at five-thirty, but by then, she'd begun to worry – she couldn't shake the sudden and deep gut feeling that told her something wasn't right.

Beverly drove the short distance to Benji's house, but as soon as she turned onto his block she knew he wasn't home – his driveway was conspicuously empty. Following her instincts, she changed her tactics and set out for Fort Griffin.

As she made the fifty-mile drive, she used her car's hands-free feature to try to call Benji three more times. Each was unsuccessful, and with each failed attempt her certainty that something had happened to him grew.

She was dismayed to see that Benji's truck wasn't in the nearly deserted parking lot when she pulled into Fort Griffin's main entrance. But Beverly noticed Alfred, one of the fort's caretakers, walking out to the sole remaining car, and she motioned him over.

"Hey, Alfred, I'm glad I caught you. Have you seen Benji?"

The man frowned.

"No, not since about nine o'clock. But then again we had a rainstorm come through that cancelled the entire morning schedule for us. He was supposed to be back here around one, I think, and by then I was at the back of the property, so he could have come and left again without me seeing him. Maybe he's at Phantom Hill? He mentioned that he had tours set up for both sites today."

"Oh. Well, I'm sure he's down there, then. Thanks, Alfred," Beverly replied, trying to keep her increasing unease out of her voice. "See you later."

She pulled out of the lot and drove back to the main road, then headed south toward Phantom Hill, only barely resisting the urge to floor it.

After a drive that felt like forever, Beverly turned into the tiny five-space gravel lot at Fort Phantom Hill and parked next to Benji's truck. She peeked through the driver's side window and saw his cell phone lying on the center console.

"Okay, he just left his phone, is all. He's probably out here somewhere enthralling some tourists," she told herself, and set off on the narrow gravel trail that snaked its way all around the site.

As she approached the old commissary she could see Benji sitting propped up against the wall, and at first she thought he was simply taking a break.

She called out to him, and when he didn't answer, she quickened her pace, afraid that some sort of cardiac event had rendered him unable to acknowledge her or reply.

It wasn't until she was mere feet away from him that she noticed all the blood that soaked the red plaid flannel shirt he was so fond of, and she ran, stumbling, screaming, to close the remaining distance between them.

She fell to her knees, then stripped off her jacket to try to put pressure on his wounds before she grabbed her phone out of her purse.

The nine-one-one operator who answered her panicked call

stayed on the line with a hysterical Beverly and tried his best to coach her through how to perform CPR while they both waited for help to arrive.

Time seemed to grind to a stop for her until the still, ominous air all around her filled with sirens wailing. As emergency crews closed her position, Beverly closed her eyes and prayed.

The moment she was gently shuffled out of the way so that the paramedics could tend to Benji, she dialed another number to reach out to Mack Racine, Benji's best friend.

"Racine's Bar," a deep, gruff voice answered just as she heard one of the paramedics tell another to call for the Justice of the Peace to officially pronounce death.

"Mack, it's Beverly," she sobbed. "Benji... Benji's dead."

"Where are you?"

"Phantom Hill."

"I'm on my way, sugar. Sit tight."

Within the hour, a kind, sympathetic Jones County deputy had taken Beverly's detailed statement before he subtly directed Mark Racine a few steps away to speak to him privately.

"She's in shock. You might want to take her to the hospital and get her checked out. Besides, we need to prep him for transport. She doesn't need to see that," he murmured to the bar owner, and Mack nodded his agreement.

They walked back over to Beverly and Mack gently wrapped one brawny arm around her petite shoulders.

"Come on, sugar, come with me. We'll worry about the cars later," he soothed, and guided her footsteps back along the path to where his truck was parked.

Once they'd finished taking photographs of the murder site, two other deputies scoured the area with high-powered flashlights looking for any spent cartridge casings. Meanwhile, Benji Patterson's remains were carefully placed into a body bag and loaded into a transport van destined for Fort Worth, since Jones County had no coroner's office.

Tarrant County Medical Examiner Dr. Jerry Broder was about to sit down to a late dinner after a very long day when his cell phone rang. He answered, asked two questions, then hung up and sighed.

"Gotta go back to the office, hon," he told his wife, who nodded sympathetically. "Got one coming in."

"Coming from where?"

"Abilene."

"Then you've got plenty of time to eat before you have to leave," she chided with a knowing smile. "You know as well as I do that you get cranky when you're hungry."

"You're right. Pass the potatoes, hon."

Forty minutes later, he stood and helped his wife of thirty-three years clear the table and clean the kitchen, then kissed her cheek.

"I'll be back," he said simply, and left the house to drive back to the coroner's office complex to wait for the transport van's arrival.

His patience was finally rewarded when his latest case arrived a little after eleven-thirty. Broder instructed the transport team to place the body on the center examination table.

Once the transport crew departed, Broder and his assistant carefully photographed the adult male from various angles as they removed his bloodied clothing piece by piece.

"What the..." his assistant looked over at Broder.

"What?"

His assistant held up what he'd fished out of the victim's front pocket. The moment Broder saw the looping scrawl on the envelope, he was pulling off his gloves and striding over to the desk in the corner for his cell phone.

A sleepy Nathan Thomas answered on the third ring.

"Thomas," he croaked, then cleared his throat and tried again.

"Thomas here."

"It's Dr. Broder. You need to come down here. *Now.*"

Nathan's scalp began to tingle.

"What's going on?" he asked as he sat upright in bed and glanced over at a concerned Bella.

"Another body - and another note for you."

"I'll be there in twenty," Nathan replied, and hung up.

He hurriedly pulled on clothes and his shoes, then leaned over to kiss Bella.

"Don't wait up. This could take a while."

"Just be careful, love. See you when you get back."

True to his word, twenty minutes later Nathan was standing shoulder-to-shoulder with the seasoned medical examiner.

"You know him, don't you?" the coroner asked.

"Yeah. That's Benji Patterson. He was the lone surviving shooting victim in the Texas Forts Trail case last year."

"Second one of those in less than a week, am I right?" Broder asked as he pointed to the sealed envelope lying on its own separate, miniature exam tray, and Nathan nodded.

"Damn, son," Broder mused, his expression equal parts deep thought and concern. "Someone sure does want your full attention."

"Don't I know it," Nathan replied with a frown. "I've got to get ahead of this guy and at the same time try to keep what's left of my team safe."

"What on earth are you talking about?"

Nathan sighed.

"We're being hunted, Doc. Everybody that was on that joint task force. Two people have been killed already, and Grace's car was tampered with. It exploded down in Galveston. Luckily, she wasn't hurt."

Broder's jaw dropped wide open.

"I saw that on the news, but I had no idea that the agent involved was one of yours."

"Yep," Nathan confirmed with a scowl. "And the guy targeting us is like a freaking ghost. There's been very few leads to chase. Meanwhile, I had team members that were refusing to leave even though I asked them to, repeatedly, for their own safety until just last night."

"I can't help with that piece of things. But as far as this man here and Theresa McNamara? My opinion and two dollars will buy you a Coke, but I have a theory," Broder said abruptly.

"Lay it on me."

"I don't think these notes have a damn thing to do with any of your cases. Not directly, anyway. I think this might be about *you*, Nathan. Whatever is driving this, it's personal."

"I was just thinking the same thing," Nathan replied. "Because Theresa McNamara's and Benji Patterson's lives do not intersect in any way at all, save one – they were both involved in some way in a prior case of mine."

Nathan held Broder's gaze.

"And I need to figure out why and who, because otherwise, my gut says you will get more bodies in here that include fan mail for me," he said grimly. "Can you get that letter over to Trish as soon as possible?"

"Did you want to read it before we bag and tag it?"

"Not really," Nathan grimaced, "but I will."

Nathan put on latex gloves, then carefully sliced open the bottom of the envelope so he wouldn't disturb any trace evidence along the gummed flap. He worked the single page out through the opening he'd made, unfolded it, and read it out loud.

"I hope you've missed me as much as I've missed you, Nathan. Looking forward to our next encounter. I'll be seeing you soon. Count on that. – C."

"C? For chameleon, maybe?" Broder offered. "Since unlike most serial killers, this individual doesn't seem to be married to any single method of murder. And there's no way this is a copycat. Can't be. To my knowledge, nothing about the first note was made public at all. Only the killer and law enforcement working the case know about it."

He looked over at Nathan.

"That other note didn't come through here; the techs at the McNamara scene found it and sent it straight over to Trish's lab. What did that first note say?"

"Pretty much identical to this one and it was signed the exact same way. Same handwriting, too."

"Well, then," Broder announced after a long pause. I'd say you have a secret admirer, Agent Thomas, and *not* the good kind. Be careful, son. And let me know if I can help in any way."

As a worried Nathan Thomas left the coroner's office to head back toward another sleepless night, the individual responsible for Theresa's and Benji's untimely deaths grumbled at the dire lack of more potential targets with which to gain the profiler's undivided interest.

Sighing deeply, the killer scrolled back up to the top of the search results and began again - and after checking and cross-checking the data set for another two hours and forty-five minutes, a scowl curved upward into a triumphant smile.

With a few more mouse clicks it became crystal-clear whose

deaths would be the most likely to cause Nathan Thomas to drop everything else and give chase.

Navigating to the next targets' websites answered any remaining questions regarding how to proceed. One carefully crafted email later, the murderer scrubbed a hand across bleary eyes and opted to get some long overdue sleep.

Chapter Thirteen

Donny Atherton woke a little after seven, and he chuckled softly to himself when Lizzie grumbled in her sleep before rolling over to her side in a subconscious response to his getting out of bed.

He padded sleepily down the stairs to start the coffeepot, then turned on his cell phone. His email account notification sounded immediately, and he opened the app and scrolled while he waited for the coffee to finish brewing.

The most recent email in his inbox was one that his website had auto forwarded through the 'Contact Me' page. He clicked on it and skimmed it.

Huh. Sounds like they want a full bundle of coverage...

The subtle chime of the coffeepot interrupted his train of thought.

Food first, he decided, and Donny stood to move to the counter and pour himself a cup, then grabbed eggs and bacon from the refrigerator.

He arranged slices of bacon in a skillet and turned on the burner under the pan, then turned back toward the kitchen table – and almost jumped out of his skin.

A shivering Lizzie was standing right behind him, her robe wrapped tightly around her and her sleepy eyes hopeful as she squeaked out, "Coffee?"

"Jesus, you startled me," Donny gasped, a hand on his chest. "I didn't hear you come downstairs."

"Sorry," she mumbled. "You left. It got cold."

"Yeah, it is a little brisk up here in the mornings," he admitted as he recovered enough to pour her a large mug of coffee. "Here, baby. And I'll turn the heat up a bit, too."

"Thanks," she murmured, then took a sip and grinned. "That's the stuff."

He adjusted the thermostat, then returned to the kitchen as she moved to the table, sat down, and noticed his phone.

"Working before eight? On a Sunday?"

"Killing time, is all," he answered as he busied himself at the kitchen stove. "But no, I didn't plan on diving in too deeply today. Just checking a few emails to line out my meeting schedules over the next two weeks."

He looked over his shoulder at her.

"I wonder when it will be safe for me to start meeting with my clients face-to-face again."

Lizzie shrugged before taking another, longer sip from her mug, and frowned when her own cell phone rang. She stood and disconnected it from the charger cord on the kitchen counter before she looked at the display.

"It's Nathan. I swear he never sleeps," she muttered as it continued to ring.

"And? Answer it. I know you still have heartburn about being left in the dark, Lizzie, but it could be important."

She stuck her tongue out at him and got a playful smirk in return before she answered the call with a cool, calm, "Good morning, Nathan."

When she gasped and said *"What?"* but didn't speak again for several moments, Donny turned around to watch her expression.

Her eyes cut to his, and he felt the same alarm he saw in them.

After a few minutes, she said, "Okay. Yes... Got it. See you tomorrow."

She hung up the phone and sighed.

"Okay, so, the answer to your 'is it safe yet' question is probably not. There's been another murder, and Nathan got another note."

"Who?" Donny asked, incredulous. "I mean, it was only Theresa and me left, so...".

"Different case this time. Remember the Texas Forts Trail case that Nathan was leading the work on around this time last year?"

"Yep, hard to forget that one. Identical twins separated at birth," Donny confirmed. "Sometimes truth really *is* stranger than fiction."

"Don't I know it," Lizzie agreed. "Anyway, no, this time it was Benji Patterson."

Donny's brow furrowed for a moment before he remembered.

"Was that the gruff old guy who lived out west of here?"

"With a teddy bear personality hidden underneath. Yep, that's Benji."

"I'm sorry, hon," he told her as he stirred the scrambled eggs he'd started. "I remember you saying he was feisty and fun."

Lizzie sighed.

"Yeah, I kinda liked that old coot. I wonder what the hell happened to him."

"Nathan didn't say?"

"Nope, only that he was killed. He did share something with me that Broder said, though."

"Broder? Who's that?"

"The Tarrant County coroner. Broder seems to think that whoever is killing people and leaving these notes is after Nathan."

Donny mulled that over as he turned off the burners, plated the food, and carried it over to the table.

"You mean Nathan's the real target?"

"Yes."

"I don't understand that at all. If you're after someone, why kill anybody else? Why not just go after that person directly?"

"Because," Lizzie said solemnly, "none of us think that Nathan is in any physical danger. Not yet, at least. This struck Broder almost like a deranged fan scenario – and the more I think about it, I agree."

Understanding dawned in Donny's eyes.

"Taking people out just to try and get on Nathan's radar?"

"Exactly."

"Then it could be *any* of us in his circle, Liz, not just people from his past cases," Donny pointed out. "Including you. As a matter of fact – why would someone select victims that are only tangentially connected to him *at all?*"

Lizzie's eyes went wide with realization.

"Oh, hell," she blurted out as she dropped her fork and grabbed her phone to call Nathan back.

"What?"

"Trial transcripts become part of the public record unless they're sealed by the courts. That's what his stalker is doing. Nathan's personal information is locked down; all of ours is. That's part of being on the job. They can't get to him that way, so, they're reviewing public records of the cases he's worked. None of his cases have been sealed that I know of – there was no reason to. This person is digging to try and find out more about him through the trial transcripts," she explained in a breathless rush before Nathan answered.

"Nathan, I just had a thought," she announced, read him in, and then listened for a few minutes.

When the conversation was finished, she set her phone down and looked at her husband.

"We need to get home as soon as possible," she said. "Nathan just mentioned that Annie finally wised up and got the hell out of town. That means that there is one less person around to watch his back. I need to be down there."

"We'll head out right after breakfast, then," Donny said, then turned pale.

"What's the matter?"

"Dammit. I need to check on something," he told her, and rushed away from the kitchen table to grab his laptop bag from its place on the couch.

"Donny, what's going on?"

"I think I made a really bad mistake, Lizzie," he confessed with a wince as he fired up his computer and navigated to his website.

"Right here," he said, and pointed as she came around the table to look over his shoulder.

"Babe. That's not good," Lizzie muttered.

"I know, I know. I wasn't even thinking about it being a possible security breach," he said as he logged in under his site administrator credentials. "They required an address to set this thing up and it honestly never even occurred to me that putting our home address wouldn't be a good idea."

"You need to disable that until we can get a post office box set up," she urged.

He typed rapidly, then hit 'save'.

"Okay. I just took my entire website offline for maintenance," he confirmed, then raised wary eyes to look over at her.

"I just hope that whoever killed Theresa and that Patterson guy didn't see it."

***

Down in Fort Worth, Dr. Broder put some finishing touches on the autopsy report that he'd begun the night before for Benji Patterson.

As he'd suspected, three of the four bullets used in the murder had been superfluous – the killer's shot directly through the upper left chest had been the death blow.

Unfortunately, each round had also been through-and-through. Not one fragment remained. That, coupled with the massive damage caused to the victim's body, led Broder to speculate that the caliber used was most likely a .38 or higher.

Once he'd called and confirmed with Jones County that no spent cartridges had been found onsite, he also revealed to them his belief that most likely the killer had either taken time to police his brass or used a revolver.

———

Armed with Broder's impressions of the weapon used, Jones County deputies returned to Phantom Hill and carefully examined the stone wall that Patterson's body had been resting against when he was first found.

Two of the four rounds that had traveled through him were located embedded in the rough-hewn rock roughly chest-height in the wall. Both were successfully pried free from their resting places, then bagged and tagged for transport to Trish Wallace's talented staff in Fort Worth.

By Monday afternoon Trish would verify that the weapon used to murder Benji Patterson was a .40 caliber handgun.

———

It was late mid-morning when Caleb Evans' friend and racquetball partner rang his doorbell. After waiting a few minutes, he knocked a few times, then rang the doorbell again.

When he still didn't get an answer, he huffed, then plucked his cell phone from its holster and called – and witnessed a strange, slightly delayed echoing of each ring, once through his phone's speaker, then again through Caleb's apartment door.

He left a message after the obligatory beep, shrugged his shoulders, and walked back to his truck.

———

The unknown car slowed to a crawl as the driver cross-checked the handwritten notes against each house number. Satisfied, the unexpected visitor parked at the curb and exited the vehicle to stroll casually up to the door and loudly knock, then wait, three separate times.

A deep sigh preceded the retreat to the vehicle when no one answered the door.

Could have sworn that this is Donny Atherton's address, the killer thought with a frown. *Guess I will need to check his website again. I must have written it down wrong.*

Javier took a short break from his interrogation somewhere around two o'clock.

He had successfully tracked Agent Baker out to his family's tenacre spread in rural Tarrant County. Once he was sure that only the man he sought was in residence, he knocked on the door, then knocked Patrick Baker out cold and dragged him out to the ancient, weather-worn metal barn for their impending talk.

He'd made sure that Baker's good arm and both legs were secured, then doused him with cold water and brought him around.

The next two hours had been filled with snarled questions met with stony silence, followed by blow after blow in the hopes of loosening Baker's tongue.

Now Javier stood off to one side, smoking a cigarette and giving his arms a rest.

"*Please.*"

The single word that floated across the space to him was uttered through swollen, blood-stained lips with raw, unfiltered desperation and no small amount of pain.

"I'm sorry, but the answer is no," Javier replied calmly as he took in Patrick Baker's sweaty, battered face. "It's simple, really. If you would just answer the questions, this would all end. But you refuse to cooperate with me. So, it seems we've reached a stalemate here."

Javier crushed out his cigarette, then pivoted to reach over to the rectangular metal tray he'd set up and picked up an icepick.

"Unless we try some other things next? Perhaps that is the best course of action, since every punch I've landed so far has only served to make you *more* stubborn, not less," he explained, a feral grin forming as he watched his prey's swollen shut eyes try to bulge open in terror at his words.

"I....I...".

"Here, let me help you decide," Javier soothed, and slammed the icepick into the same shoulder that he'd shattered with a bullet on the day he'd assassinated Ramon Gutierrez.

Baker's screams tore through the dilapidated barn like a rabid animal.

"Annie... Bianca is Annie," Baker finally confessed on a sob.

"Annie *Adams*?"

"Yes... Adams...," Baker mumbled.

A few more questions, and Javier was satisfied.

"See, that wasn't so hard, was it?" Javier scoffed as he moved around behind the man he'd strapped to a chair. "Thank you for your cooperation. You can go now."

Patrick Baker began to babble his thanks, but his words stopped mid-stream as Javier pressed his gun's muzzle to the back of Baker's head and squeezed the trigger.

Javier calmly secured his weapon, retrieved the casing, then packed up his small assortment of tools and left the barn.

"Annie Adams, huh?" he said as he slid back behind the wheel of the Land Rover and looked at himself in the rear-view mirror. "Back to Grace's apartment, then."

As Donny and Lizzie's flight home landed at Dallas Fort Worth International Airport, a harried complex maintenance worker who was running way behind schedule knocked briefly on Caleb Evans' door.

"Maintenance," he called out. "I'm here to change out your air filters."

When no one responded, he huffed, then used his master key to let himself in, and swapped out the filter in the living room, setting the old one down by the front door.

He picked up the second new filter allocated for unit 104 and made his way into the bedroom.

But the sight that greeted him made him retch and gag, and he stumbled backward out of the room, then turned and fled all the way out to the sidewalk.

He dialed emergency services and managed to give them his name and the address before he lost the battle to control his stomach.

Patrick Baker's mom and dad arrived home around six p.m. from their fun-filled Sunday spent antiquing and were surprised to see that while his truck was still in the driveway, their son was nowhere to be found in the house.

Ever since he'd been shot, they had worried about him – particularly when the doctors told him that he'd be unable to return to active duty as a federal agent. The resultant depression that their only child had fallen into had made it nearly impossible for either of them to even get him to accompany them into town.

"Maybe a friend came by and picked him up, honey," his father said, and patted her arm. "You keep saying that he needs to stop shutting himself away."

"I know I do," his mother replied. "It's not healthy for him to just wander around this house like a ghost. He's only thirty-six, for crying out loud."

She looked around the kitchen.

"Still, you would think he'd have left a note."

His father shuffled to the refrigerator to get the pitcher of tea. As he did, he glanced out the window that faced the back of the property and frowned.

"Huh. Barn door's open," he observed.

"Maybe he's puttering around out there," his wife replied. "It'd be a start, at least."

"I'll go check. I need to unload that cedar chest that you couldn't live without anyway," he told her with a grin.

He kissed her cheek before he headed back outside to his truck and pulled it around the side of the house and over to the little storage shed next to the barn.

He unlocked the shed, then hefted the chest up and carried it inside, padlocking the pull-down door behind him again when he was done. Then he turned toward the barn.

Within moments, he'd called nine-one-one for help.

His wife heard his frantic shouts from inside the house, and she raced out the back door and toward the barn.

Patrick's father closed the distance to her about halfway between the two buildings and held her tightly to stop her forward motion.

"No, honey. *No.* You don't want to see that," he urged her with tear-filled eyes. "You really don't. Stay right here with me."

Chapter Fourteen

Nathan and Lizzie both arrived at work on Monday morning only minutes before a solemn director summoned them both to join him in his office.

This must be about my leaving abruptly on Friday, she thought, and grimaced.

She walked with them both, a tense, uncomfortable silence weighing down her every step, and the director waved her and Nathan through the open door before he closed it and sat down behind his desk. Lizzie and Nathan took their seats in the director's visitors' chairs placed directly across from him.

"Are you all right, sir?" Lizzie asked as she took in the director's haggard yet furious expression.

"In a word, no. The DEA's director was waiting for me the moment I stepped off the elevator this morning. There's been two more deaths."

Lizzie's eyebrows raised, and she noticed that to her right, Nathan tucked his chin and closed his eyes.

"Who?" he asked softly.

"DEA Agents Caleb Evans and Patrick Baker."

"*Baker?*" Lizzie exclaimed. "But he wasn't anywhere near the restaurant, sir."

"I'm well aware of that, Agent Zimmerman, and I'm just as surprised as you are on that one."

"What happened to them?" Nathan interjected.

"Both shot with a large caliber weapon at close range," came the terse reply. "The coroner estimates that Evans died sometime early Saturday morning, but his body wasn't found until yesterday afternoon. Agent Baker's body was discovered by his father yesterday around six p.m. and the coroner believes his time of death occurred four to six hours before he was found."

"Any other evidence?"

The director sighed.

"Yes. Evans' body had no physical trauma other than his gunshot wounds. Baker, on the other hand, had been beaten all to hell before he was executed."

"He was tortured," Nathan murmured, and the director nodded.

"That's exactly how Broder phrased it, yes."

Nathan looked at the director, then at Lizzie, then back again.

"The only two agents left from the restaurant op, at least as far as Javier knows, are Hank and Annie," he began. "And yes, Baker wasn't onsite the night Ramon was picked up, but he *was* part of the transport team. I think Javier connected those dots and worked Baker over for information as to who "Bianca" really is."

"That's right. Agent Adams *was* undercover for that op," the director recalled. "Which would have left him little to nothing to go on."

"Sir, we have to assume that Baker broke under torture and gave Javier whatever information he wanted," Nathan declared. "While Annie's already left town, I think we need to warn her that Javier is very capable of closing her position – especially if he now knows her real name."

"Agreed. I know we're supposed to keep a certain secret, Agent Thomas, but I'm fed up. Being muzzled like we have been has done nothing except get more agents killed. I'm sick and tired of it, and it stops, right now."

He turned his gaze to Lizzie.

"So let me read you in, Agent Zimmerman. Almost four years ago the DEA boys up in Washington had this bright idea to put one of their guys directly into the cartel's path on purpose. This individual was meant to infiltrate the cartel's ranks by offering to be their 'inside man' in the DEA, but his *real* mission was to gather as much intel as possible so that they could dismantle the Cortinas cartel from the inside when the time came."

"Why do I get the feeling that something went very wrong with their brilliant plan," Lizzie muttered.

"Because that's exactly what happened, in the worst way imaginable. Cesar Nelson slipped his DEA handler's leash - and then he disappeared without a trace. For the last two years, they've believed him to be dead."

The director paused long enough to lean forward and rest his arms on his desk.

"You two probably know him better as Javier, the mechanic from the garage videos."

Nathan's jaw dropped, and Lizzie snapped her head his direction.

"You didn't know that either, Nathan?" she asked, her voice trembling.

"Agent Thomas was left out of that part of this loop. We were only told that one of theirs had gone rogue and that they were dealing with it internally. Even *I* didn't know that Javier and Nelson were one and the same until about a half-hour ago, when I learned that two more agents had been murdered and I finally lost my temper. If we'd known who he really was, there would have been a hell of a lot more security present on that transport detail. I'd have made sure of *that*," the director snarled.

"So, Javier, or Nelson, or whatever he's calling himself these days.

He's..." Lizzie's face was pale, and her voice faltered as her mind reeled with the implications.

"Fully trained, including military special forces before he signed on with the DEA. He's completely lethal. And evidently, a complete traitor, as well. The DEA director thinks - and I agree - that it isn't just what's left of the task force at risk anymore. *No one* here is safe."

"What's the plan, sir?" she asked.

"This part, we *did* already know," the director prefaced, then continued, "They've sent Hank Myers after him."

"Why Myers?"

"Evidently, they have the same background. The same training. From what I was told this morning, he and Nelson even went on some of the same missions. If anybody can get the drop on Nelson, it's Myers."

"So, Hank is going undercover to flush this guy out?"

At the director's nod, Nathan fielded her question.

"No, Lizzie. Not to flush him out. Hank Myers was sent out to hunt him down and kill him. *That* is his mission."

He glanced over at the director.

"And now that we know the full truth about *why* Hank was chosen, that directive makes a lot more sense."

A long, solemn silence permeated the room before the director cleared his throat.

"As there's nothing left to say on that topic, let's move on to other business while you're both here. Agent Thomas, what's the status on the McNamara murder?"

"There's been no forward progress as far as identifying her killer, and now a second victim has surfaced. Benji Patterson."

The director's face scrunched in confusion.

"From the Texas Forts Trail case?"

"Yes, sir."

"Same weapon?"

"No, sir. Theresa McNamara was beaten. Benji Patterson was

shot. But Broder found a note on Patterson's body that was addressed to me."

"Two notes now. I see," Nathan's boss replied smoothly. "And when do *you* plan to go off the grid?"

"Beg pardon?"

"One murder that ties back to an old case of yours could be written off as a coincidence. But now you're telling me that there's two of them. I think we seriously need to consider the possibility that the real target could be *you*."

"I concur," Lizzie said. "And from what you told me yesterday, Nathan, even Dr. Broder has the same opinion."

"I - I can't just *leave*, sir," Nathan stammered. "I have what's left of a team to run and cases to solve here. How is my leaving going to solve anything? I need to look through the rest of my old cases and identify potential targets. If I can get even one step ahead, I can catch this guy. I know I can."

"I'm aware of all that, Agent Thomas. For the record, my gut says I should bench you for your own safety."

Nathan started to speak but the director held up his hand for silence.

"But, I'm *also* all too aware that you're just stubborn enough to strike out on your own regardless of what I say. So, for now, I'm keeping you active."

"Thank you, sir."

"One caveat. You do not go *anywhere* alone. Agent Zimmerman is your new best friend – and bodyguard."

The director pivoted his gaze in Lizzie's direction.

"You good with that, Agent Zimmerman?"

"Yes, sir, I am."

"Good. Now, I suggest you two go iron out whatever differences you seem to be having lately so that you can both focus on the task at hand. Dismissed."

Nathan and Lizzie opted to move to his office to do as the director suggested and clear the air between them.

The moment his office door was shut he said, "I know you're mad."

"I was," Lizzie admitted. "Not anymore. I understand why you guys kept that from me. Quite frankly, if our roles had been reversed, I'd have done the same. And you were right – now that I know…".

Her voice trailed off and she shrugged.

"But my anger isn't at you or Joe or Rick anymore. That's not where it belongs. Lenny Kennard is who I should have been upset with the moment I found out. It wasn't fair to any of you that you had to try to shield me from all that. That's on him and him alone."

"So, we're good?"

"We're good," she assured him. "Okay, so, now that we have that cleared up, how do you want to proceed here? Keep looking at your past cases?"

"Yes," Nathan confirmed. "But first we need to make a couple of calls. Annie and Hank both need to know about Evans and Baker – and Annie needs to be told who Javier really is."

"I'll reach out to Annie. And I don't know about you, but I could use some coffee. Want some?" she offered.

"You really have to ask me that?" he teased. "Wow. And here I thought we were friends. It's like you don't even know me."

She laughed. "Touché. I'll be right back."

<hr>

At home in Pantego, Donny poured himself a cup of coffee and began his workday in earnest. Several more emails had arrived since he'd last looked at his laptop on Sunday morning.

He scrolled to the bottom of the unread messages to work on them in the order received. Before long, he was clicking on and reading the inquiry that had been sent through his website.

He scanned the message's contents, then hit 'reply'.

Hello and thanks for reaching out. I can certainly assist with putting together the quotes that you've expressed an interest in. Unfortunately, I am not currently doing in-person consultations, but if you like I'm happy to schedule a video conference with you. Just let me know your preferred days and times and we'll make it happen.

He signed off with his updated signature block - one that did *not* include his physical address anymore - and hit 'send', then opened the next email.

Up at the lake house, Annie's brows knitted with worry as she listened to Lizzie's update.

"They think that Baker was tortured for information about *me?*"

"That's the theory."

"I...I don't even know what to say to that. How could someone be so cruel?"

She heard Lizzie's deep sigh.

"I don't know, Annie. The kind of mindset it would take to be able to even *think* of something like that... I can barely wrap my head around it, either."

"So, it's down to just us two now. Me and Hank."

"For now, yes."

"What do you mean, 'for now'?"

"Both directors believe he's a real threat to everyone in this branch office, not just the joint task force."

"Do Nathan or the director have any thoughts about what Javier's... I mean, Nelson's next move might be?"

"If they do, they didn't tell me. We just wanted you to have all the information. Stay put and keep your head down, okay? Hank's hunting this guy."

"Seriously?" Hank asked when Nathan told him what the rogue DEA agent had done to Baker. "That's low, even for him."

"I'll have to take your word for it, since you know this guy," Nathan replied, his tone clipped.

"I'm sorry, man. I could only reveal so much."

"I know. I'm not upset with you. I'm just tired of the big bosses and their cloak and dagger bullshit. At least it's all out in the open now, and knowledge is power."

"Speaking of – since I know how Cesar Nelson operates," Hank chimed in. "He'll target Annie next, and probably grab her to lure me out. I can guarantee you that he wants the grand finale to be me; that's just the kind of egotistical asshole he is. He never bested me anytime we went head-to-head back in special ops, so he's got a huge chip on his shoulder where I'm concerned. He will try to use her as bait to get to me and stack the odds in his favor while he's at it."

"How do we counter that?"

"I'll be in place already when he shows up to grab her," Hank revealed. "Matter of fact, I'm about to head her way. I won't be able to contact her, though. I'll only get one shot at putting him down, so I'll have to stay in the shadows. But if Nelson does what he always does, he'll dig like hell until he gets her location, then he'll go in guns blazing. He's never been one to choose subtlety when brute force is an option."

When Grace's nosy neighbor proved to be a hindrance on Sunday afternoon, Javier, aka Cesar Nelson, had reluctantly decided to retreat and try again the following day.

He watched from a distance as the busybody neighbor left for work. Once he was confident the coast was clear, he sauntered up the sidewalk, jamming the building's exterior cameras as he went, then picked the lock and quietly eased himself into Grace's apartment.

Nelson immediately picked up the stack of mail addressed to

Annie Adams and rifled through it. He peeled back the temporary forwarding labels to take pictures of two different pre-printed addresses that appeared in the mix of junk mail and bills.

Huh. Neither address is a very long drive from here... I'd better check out both.

He tidied up the stack and set it down again where he'd found it on the kitchen counter, then out of habit made one last circuit through the unit to verify he hadn't missed any potential clues that could help him track Annie.

As he did, Nelson pondered the best way to investigate each address directly without arousing suspicion.

I need to be able to not just gain access but have an excuse to refuse to deal with anyone but her...

He smiled as the ideal cover persona came to him.

Process server. It's perfect.

"Better get moving, then," he muttered as he cracked Grace's front door open just wide enough to check that he wasn't being watched. "I've got to pick up some supplies."

He stepped out, locked the door behind him, and headed for his Land Rover. His first stop was an office supply store, and the next was to a beauty supply outlet before he headed back to Ramon's place.

"Time to change things up," he said to his reflection in his bathroom mirror as he picked up the electric razor he'd purchased. "The scruffy look has to go."

Meanwhile, Lizzie and Nathan had moved to the conference room, where the official, printed copies of Nathan's previous cases had been stacked in a row on the credenza.

"I think it's safe to say that the Kennard files are tapped out," he mused as she booted up her laptop.

Even as she nodded her agreement she replied, "Yes, but I *also* don't think we need to worry about digging into the majority of those other files just yet."

"Why is that?"

"Well for starters, some of your other cases never went to trial," she answered, and ticked names off on her fingers as she listed them.

"Mikel Metzger fled the country, D.A. Rogers committed suicide, Dr. Jamesin was shot to death in open court on the second day, and the two that wreaked havoc out at Lighte's Landing haven't even been *scheduled* for trial yet."

"You're right. Which means that there *is* no public record for my stalker to sift through. Guess we're focusing on the Stephen Walsh case next."

"Yep. That, and we need to look at your background. We can't rule out the possibility that this lunatic is someone you already know."

"I've had that thought too," he muttered through his frown, "and that may mean going back a ways. I was a Virginia State Trooper before I joined the FBI. This could be someone with a grudge that dates back years."

His smile was half-hearted.

"You should be the one to dig through my background for clues, Liz. You might pick up on some things that I might miss because I'm just too close to it. I'll revisit the Walsh case."

"You got it. We also need to update Joe – and I think we should tell him to at least watch his back if he won't alter his schedule. Until this person is caught, all four of us need to be on guard, just in case."

He pulled his cell phone out of its holster.

"I couldn't agree more, Liz. I'll call him now. Donny's still taking precautions, right?"

"Yep," she confirmed. "He's only doing online meetings with clients until this is over. I do need to tell you one thing, though."

Nathan paused his navigation to Joe's number to glance up at her.

"By the look on your face, it isn't good."

"No, it's not," she admitted, "but I'm hoping it was caught in time. Donny wasn't thinking when he set up his website, and he used our home address. He's taken it offline until we can get him a post office box, but there's no way to know if your biggest fan saw it or not. He's able to track general data about how many visitors his site gets, but that's it."

"Well. Now I have a *second* reason to call Rick Conner and get him involved," Nathan announced, "because if anyone can track that data down to a specific person, it's him."

"What's the first reason?"

"Dallas PD managed to refine some video from the nightclub. We have a license plate number for a Land Rover - and the guy driving it looked a lot like Nelson, according to Hank. I want Rick to help wade through traffic camera activity and see if we can't spot the same vehicle other places. Maybe we can rule the driver of the Land Rover out as a suspect, or even better, catch a break and trace Nelson back to his nest before he even has a chance to get to Annie."

He resumed his search for Joe's number and placed the first call, then put it on speakerphone and set it down on the table between him and Lizzie.

"Hey, Joe. You got a minute? Lizzie and I have some updates for you."

The individual hoping to lure Donny Atherton out into the open read his emailed response and scowled.

Dammit. How can I get to him if he won't meet up in person? Need to think about that some more. In the meantime, I guess I'll have to go with option B...

A few minutes later the killer had successfully booked an intake appointment through Joe Wallace's secretary for ten a.m. Tuesday morning.

Once he'd read Joe in, Nathan reached out to Rick Conner. He had to leave a voicemail, but he didn't have to wait very long for Rick to respond.

"What's up?" Rick asked when he returned Nathan's call.

"I've got Lizzie here with me, and you're on speakerphone," Nathan responded. "I find myself in need once again of your superior tech."

"Do tell."

"This request has two parts. First, we need to get specifics on anyone that's viewed both Donny Atherton's and Joe Wallace's websites in, say, the last three weeks."

"That's an oddly specific request. Are they having trouble with somebody?"

With a sigh, Nathan relayed the highlights, ending with, "Until this person is caught all four of us – me, Lizzie, Donny, and Joe – are potential targets."

Rick was silent for a long moment.

"I'll go over to Donny and Lizzie's place here shortly and get that started on his computer, and I'll call Joe and coordinate with him once you and I are done talking. What's the other task you need done?"

"I need to know more about where a certain vehicle's been traveling in the Dallas-Fort Worth area."

"We have a tracker on the vehicle?"

"Nope," Nathan confirmed. "Just the make, model, and license plate."

"Don't want much, do you?" Rick said with a chuckle. "Trying to find his hideout?"

"Yep."

"Hmm. Difficult, but not impossible. Just may take a bit is all. What's the timeframe?"

"The sooner the better, Rick. He's actively hunting my task force team. Four confirmed deaths so far, and he tried to kill Grace Womack by blowing up her car. Luckily, she wasn't in it."

Nathan and Lizzie both flinched at Rick's bellowed "*What?*"

Nathan sighed once again, then read Rick into the situation his team was facing with the cartel.

"*Jesus,*" the IT specialist exclaimed. "Let me make sure that I have this right. You're under attack from *two different* directions at once?"

"Yes."

"You need to email me all the information you have on that car and on any locations he might have visited as soon as possible. I need *all* of it – including any footage you can get your hands on. I can start a search to run in the background before I head over to see Donny. Anything else?"

Lizzie tapped some keys, then gave Nathan a thumbs-up and rotated her laptop so he could see the screen.

"Not that I'm aware of currently - and Lizzie just sent you the data on the Land Rover, the address of each murder site, and two video files. One's from the nightclub, and the other is from the parking garage where Grace's car exploded. Thanks, Rick. We appreciate it."

"I'll be in touch," he answered, and abruptly hung up.

Nathan and Lizzie exchanged glances.

"He sounded very, very pissed off," he said.

"Yes, he certainly did. Aren't you glad it's not at us again?" she answered, referring to the one and only time that either of them had borne witness to Rick losing his temper.

"Nah. Back then he just raised his volume a little to get through to us both before we came to blows in his living room," Nathan clarified. "What you heard just now? *That's* his 'pissed-to-his-core' voice."

Chapter Fifteen

Rick Conner was up for good at three-forty a.m. after trying and failing to sleep.

He'd spent the rest of his Monday setting up a program on Donny's and Joe's websites that would auto-feed metrics data over to his primary terminal for collation and deeper analysis.

Then he'd opened the email Lizzie had sent and generated a whole new set of parameters on his second terminal to cast a net for the mysterious Land Rover and its driver.

After that, he'd had dinner and watched a movie with Faith, then gone to bed. But sleep hadn't come, and the more he'd thought about everything Nathan had shared with him, the angrier he'd become.

Determined, he stalked from the bedroom into the living room, sat at his desk, and plugged in then turned on his encrypted laptop.

"You have the nerve to hunt down *my* family and friends? Game on, buddy. Let's see how you like *this*," he growled as his login window appeared.

For three solid hours he carefully prepared his counterattacks, then pressed 'enter' and stood to go make coffee while his laptop's specially enhanced programming began the search for his prey.

Joe Wallace and Pete Jenkins' usual morning meeting kicked off promptly at seven-thirty a.m.

"I noticed Madge booked a new client for me for ten o'clock this morning," Joe remarked with a wry smile. "Guess I forgot to tell her that I'd already arranged to travel offsite for a follow-up visit with a client at nine-forty-five. Can you handle meeting with the intake client for me?"

Pete grinned. "Sure, happy to. You know she's going to fuss at you for forgetting again, don't you?"

"As she should," Joe admitted. "Anyway - here's the info sheet she put together. Client's name is Sam H. Thannato, and it sounds like a case of suspected infidelity."

Pete rolled his eyes. "*Another* one? Man, why do people even bother to get into relationships if they're just going to cheat anyway?"

Joe shrugged his shoulders. "Who knows what they're thinking. But at the rate new clients are heading our way for that very reason, I think it's safe to say our jobs are secure."

Nathan and Lizzie reconvened in the conference room to continue their search for clues leading to the identity of the killer whose target seemed to be Nathan himself. As they had the day before, he focused on the Stephen Walsh files while Lizzie continued to dig into Nathan's past.

Sam H. Thannato arrived ten minutes early and was greeted by Joe's secretary – but further conversation was interrupted by a ringing phone. The woman manning the desk mimed to Sam to take a thin stack of papers and have a seat as she fielded three phone calls in rapid succession. After taking a chair in the lobby to complete the paperwork, Thannato overheard some interesting advice during one of those calls.

"Yes, well, it's public record, you know," the secretary said to whoever she was on the phone with. "Yep, I'm positive. Simple search on the county tax assessor's site would be my first suggestion... You're welcome. Have a great day."

Good to know. Might come in handy...

Once she ended the third call, Madge glanced over at the client she'd originally booked for Joe.

"I'm so sorry," she said. "What I was about to tell you before the phone began to ring was that I didn't realize it when you and I spoke yesterday, but Mr. Wallace already had a prior engagement scheduled this morning. But his associate, Mr. Jenkins, is available to meet with you."

"When *will* Mr. Wallace be available? Because I'd much rather deal with him directly," came the snarled response.

Madge's eyebrows lifted but she remained silent as she scrolled through Joe's calendar on her computer.

"I'm afraid he doesn't have any other openings for the next three weeks. The first available is May twentieth."

"Never mind, then. I'll find someone else," Thannato growled, then rose, handed back the half-finished paperwork, and stomped out of the building.

"What the hell..." Madge muttered under her breath as she picked up her phone's handset and dialed Pete's extension.

"Never mind about the Thannato intake, it's been cancelled," Pete heard Madge say.

"You okay?"

"No, actually. That was a very weird and rude encounter just now."

"What happened?"

Madge read him in, and he whistled in surprise.

"Yeah... that *is* a little weird. How far did Thannato get with the onboarding paperwork?"

"About halfway."

"Bring that to me, would you please?"

"Um, sure. I'll be right there. After I take this new call, that is."

Over in Dallas, a determined Nelson arrived at the second known address for Annie Adams.

The first he'd tried had been a complete bust. After he'd finally managed to work his way past an uncooperative receptionist to speak directly with the property manager, he'd been told that Annie was no longer a resident.

He'd muttered under his breath after he'd thanked the property manager and retreated to his vehicle.

"Could've saved me a good ten minutes if she'd actually *wanted* to be helpful," Nelson fumed, referring to the stubborn receptionist.

He used the fifteen-minute drive to try and heel his temper and managed to wrestle it back into submission as he turned into the second complex's visitor parking lot.

After he parked, he made sure that the realistic-looking employee nameplate he'd modeled after an actual process server company in the area was still securely clipped to his shirt's left front pocket. Then he grabbed his clipboard and the slender, legal-sized manila envelope filled with blank pages that served as his fake court paperwork.

"Here goes nothing," he muttered as he exited his Land Rover and walked up to the apartment community's leasing office.

The moment he entered the premises he could tell that unlike his experience with the previous receptionist, this individual would be much more cooperative – and from the way the perky blonde smiled at him, maybe even a bit gossipy, if he played his cards right.

He smiled his most charming smile and sauntered over to her desk, taking note of the small wooden nameplate as he did so.

"Good morning, Noelle," he purred. "May I call you Noelle?"

"Good morning, yourself," she purred back as she raked her gaze slowly down his body and back up to his face.

Nelson knew she liked what she saw when her smile ratcheted up a notch.

"You may. And what brings you in today?"

Nelson held up the manila envelope. "Duty calls, I'm afraid."

He paused to read the fake label he'd attached to the envelope.

"I'm trying to locate someone. Annie Adams."

"Sure, one moment, honey."

She didn't ask him for identification. She didn't even inquire as to his purpose for standing in her office. Instead, with barely a glance at his name tag, Noelle immediately began to type on her computer keyboard. In most other scenarios he'd have been mortified at the lack of data security, but today? Today, he reveled in her complete disregard for confidentiality.

"I'm so sorry. We don't have any residents here by that name currently. But hang on, let me look one more place," she said, and typed some more.

After a few moments, she grinned.

"Yep, that's what I thought. I thought that name sounded familiar. She used to live here but she moved out..."

Her voice trailed off as she looked around nervously before she whispered, "After her boyfriend was killed. So sad. They made such a cute couple."

"That's horrible," Nelson commiserated, and made sure to make his voice sound as sympathetic as possible. "What happened?"

Noelle glanced around again before she leaned forward and gave him a view straight down her low-cut blouse as she whispered, "Well, he was some sort of federal agent, and he was shot to death about a month ago. It was all over the news."

"Oh, I think I saw some clips about that," Nelson told her, then pretended to search his memory. "I can't remember his name, though...".

"It was Ben. Ben Tinsing," Noelle volunteered, then nodded solemnly.

The man in the front passenger seat was Annie Adam's live-in boyfriend? Holy shit. I think I just struck gold...

A few more questions combined with a flirtatious look netted him the forwarding address that Annie Adams had given to the front office when she moved out the week before Ben's death.

That address? Grace Womack's.

Nelson could barely contain his excitement.

"Thanks, darlin, you've been very, very helpful," he told her with a smile and a lascivious wink. "I'll see you around, then. Maybe we could get a drink sometime?"

"I'd like that."

He left a beaming Noelle behind as he made his way back out to his Land Rover.

"Wow," he said as he fastened his seatbelt. "That woman's a walking talking security breach. I cannot believe she shared so many details with a stranger. No one who lives in that complex is safe."

He looked at himself in his rearview mirror.

"I'd tell her boss – if I really cared."

Grinning, he started his car's engine, then backed out of the space.

Time to go back to Ramon's and dig into Ben Tinsing's world too, he decided.

Upon overhearing Joe Wallace's receptionist's advice to another client about public records searches, Sam H. Thannato had decided to take a more direct route to achieve the goal of a face-to-face encounter with Nathan Thomas. Stomping out of Joe Wallace's business in a fit of anger had merely been for show.

As a result, Sam arrived back at the hotel room with a renewed sense of purpose. After shedding the suit jacket and cracking open a beer, Sam turned the laptop back on and got to work in earnest.

Hank Myers pulled up in front of the tiny cabin and heaved a sigh of relief.

Once he'd realized exactly where the tracker on Annie's car had led him, he'd scrambled to find suitable accommodations that would allow him to keep watch over her but remain out of her line of sight. Fortunately, it was still early enough in the year that a few of the privately-owned cabins dotted along the northern part of Lake Texoma weren't fully booked yet.

A few extra hundred-dollar bills to sweeten the deal didn't hurt, either, he acknowledged with a grin as he exited his truck and carried his duffel bag toward the cabin's front door.

Once inside, he set his bag down and looked around – easily done from the doorway, as the cabin he was calling home for the foreseeable future was mostly one big room, with a tiny bathroom walled off for privacy. But the full-sized bed had clean, crisp sheets, and the entire place was tidy and well-organized.

Six strides carried him to the full-sized refrigerator and two overhead cabinets on either side of it. As the property owner had mentioned, there was a generous supply of coffee, creamer, and sugar - and not much else in the way of food. But the little cabin *was* fully stocked with plates, mugs, silverware, and cookware.

"Now to go check out the view," he murmured.

He stepped out the door and strolled around the side of the little log structure to make his way down the private dock.

Hank walked slowly and made detailed mental notes of his

surroundings. When he reached the end of the dock, he looked to his left, and smiled.

The cabin he'd rented was on a small cove, and he could clearly see Annie's family place about one hundred yards away down the slightly curved shoreline – just enough distance that with luck she wouldn't see him, but close enough that he'd be able to monitor things.

Of course, he thought with a grin, *the sensors I placed at their gate and down either side of their driveway will help, too.*

He glanced down at the fourteen-foot-long aluminum fishing boat that was tied to the dock. It came complete with a five-horsepower outboard motor and forty-pound thrust trolling motor in addition to a pair of oars, and the property owner had mentioned he could use it during his stay.

And now I have another way to get to her, as well.

He looked again at the distance between the two docks and calculated in his head.

I need to place more sensors in case Nelson opts to come in on foot or by water. That's the way I'd approach if it were my mission.

Satisfied that his battle plans to protect Annie were as solid as they could be given the distance, Hank headed back to the car he'd borrowed to unload the three bags of food he'd brought with him to the cabin. Once his supplies were properly stowed, he went back out and retrieved his tactical gear from the trunk.

After that, he carried his duffel bag over to the bed long enough to move his clothes into the tall, narrow, three-drawer dresser.

Then he sat at the two-person dinette table with his laptop, pulled up the map he'd saved earlier, and began to plot out exactly how the sensors he'd need to install come sunset should be placed for maximum coverage.

It wasn't until almost three o'clock that Madge appeared in his doorway with the paperwork Pete Jenkins had asked for.

"Sorry," she said sheepishly when he grinned at her. "I couldn't really get away from my desk until just now. Seems like everyone and their brother needs a private investigator lately."

"That's all right, Madge. For us, that's a good problem to have. And I got caught up in other stuff anyway," Pete reassured her. "I'll look at these shortly. I need to finish up some notes on the Parker case."

In Dallas, Lizzie paused, then grabbed her notepad and wrote down a sixth name that had caught her eye. She opened a new browser window so she could run multiple searches at once, then went back to the files she'd printed copies of and placed a small post-it note along the long edge of each page where she'd seen the newest name.

"You find something?" Nathan asked after he glanced over and saw the growing stack of pages marked with little yellow sticky notes that she was continuing to add to.

"Not sure yet. I'll let you know," she replied.

"What is it? Maybe I can answer it for you."

She set down her pen and looked over at her boss and friend.

"You chiming in on it defeats the purpose of *me* looking at all this and not you," she pointed out. "Fresh eyes and unbiased view, remember? Now, is there anything in the Walsh case that's popped for you yet?"

"Not yet," he said with a frown as his phone rang.

"Thomas."

"Hey, honey," he heard Bella say in a voice full of concern. "The daycare just called. Charlie's running a fever, and I can't leave. My final exam in French starts in like, eight minutes. Can you pick him up?"

"On my way. Good luck on your test, you got this, baby," Nathan told her, then hung up.

"Charlie's running a temperature. I've got to go get him," he informed Lizzie.

"Okay, then. Let me save my work and log off this laptop right quick and we'll get going."

"You don't need to come with me, Liz. I'm going to the daycare, then straight home. It's not like I'm heading into battle or anything."

She arched an eyebrow.

"What part of the director saying *you do not go anywhere alone* did you not get?"

Nathan huffed. "Fine."

"Don't 'fine' me," she chided. "You may not fear the director, but I do, a little bit. He can be very intimidating when he's mad."

Nathan chuckled at her honesty.

"Just so you know, I agree one hundred percent. I'd hate to see him completely lose his temper. I don't think anyone would survive it."

Sam's lips curved into a smile. The research so diligently undertaken had revealed a wealth of information – including the fact that Nathan Thomas co-owned property in Pantego, Texas with one Bella Amsel Thomas. Further searches had confirmed that Bella and Nathan had one child together, a three-year-old boy named Charles Daniel Thomas.

After a few stretches to work the kinks out from sitting still for too long, Sam diligently began to plan next steps to get Nathan's full attention once and for all.

Chapter Sixteen

On Wednesday morning Lizzie spoke with Nathan by phone. Charlie's fever had continued through the night and as a result, Nathan was spending his day tending to his son and working from home while Bella traveled to campus to complete the last two final exams of her master's degree program.

Satisfied that her boss was secured, Lizzie poured herself an oversized cup of coffee, then headed to the conference room and fired up her laptop.

In the cabin closest to Annie's, Hank Myers yawned as he made himself a breakfast sandwich and poured another cup of coffee.

His sensor-setting activities had lasted well past sundown, after which he'd trudged back toward his cabin in the pitch black aided by night-vision goggles. Once he'd returned to the privacy of his temporary residence, Hank had fired up the laptop and verified that each sensor was online and working properly before he finally opted for sleep around two in the morning.

At three-eighteen a.m. an alarm sounded – the very one he'd set his laptop to make should any of the motion-activated sensors be disturbed. He'd rushed out of bed and over to the laptop to see a magnificent twelve-point buck pawing the ground close enough to a sensor to activate it before disappearing into the surrounding brush. Hank continued watching the playback, but the animal hadn't damaged the unit and nothing else was amiss, so he'd returned to bed.

Now, a little over four hours later, he carried his sandwich and coffee mug back over to the two-person table and reviewed the sensors again.

Sam had planned to discreetly shadow Bella Thomas as she dropped Charlie off at the daycare, then stick around to try and get a better view of Nathan's little boy. But Bella walked out of the house and drove away without her son.

A curious Sam put the car into drive and followed, interested to find out where Bella Thomas was headed.

One city over, Cesar Nelson was steeped in frustration.

His search through Ben Tinsing's life and social media history had indeed turned up one slightly fuzzy photograph of the couple, but not much new information about Annie Adams besides the fact that she was possibly a natural brunette, not a blonde.

"Think, dammit. Think," he growled to himself as he paced. "There's got to be somewhere else I can look…".

He stopped mid-stride as his thoughts about Annie's hair color immediately caused an image of another blonde to pop into his head – busty, beautiful, loose-lipped Noelle.

"Looks like I'm following through on that meet-for-a-drink offer, after all," he smirked as he dialed the main phone number for Annie's old apartment complex.

A few minutes and a couple of well-told lies later, he hung up with a gushing Noelle and retreated to the bedroom to select appropriate clothes for his impromptu date that evening.

At her parents' cabin, Annie stretched, then sighed before she slowly climbed out of bed. She looked at the clock on her bedside table and frowned when she realized it was already half-past nine.

"All this sitting around doing nothing is making me lazy," she grumbled as she grabbed fresh clothes and made her way down the hall for a shower.

Her mood improved slightly by the time she'd dressed and dried her hair, and she ventured out into the fully stocked kitchen in search of breakfast.

"Morning, sweetheart," her mom said. "Did you sleep well?"

"Almost too well," Annie quipped, a wan smile stretching across her features. "And it's making me lazy. I hate this waiting game we're playing."

"Now, now, Annie-bug," her father chimed in. "I know it's not in your nature to just stand by but in this case, you know it's the smart thing to do."

Annie sighed. "I know, Dad. I'm just frustrated, is all."

By mid-morning, Lizzie was able to mark through two of the six names on her list of people from Nathan's past – Angie Sophir and Brady Tavert. Nathan had tangled with the couple during his time with the Virginia State Troopers.

When Nathan had attempted to arrest him for drunk driving, Tavert had become belligerent and punched him in the jaw.

Assaulting a peace officer had been tacked on to charges of drunk driving, disorderly conduct, and resisting arrest.

"He'd be a great one to take a closer look at for all this... if he was still alive, that is," Lizzie muttered.

She'd discovered to her surprise that Tavert had been let out on bail. While awaiting trial, he had evidently opted *not* to learn from his experiences. He'd been killed in a single-car drunk driving accident a mere two weeks before he was supposed to appear in front of the judge.

According to Lizzie's research, Angie Sophir had managed to get her life together after the night she and her then-boyfriend came across Nathan's path. All evidence pointed to Angie living contentedly in Edinburgh, Scotland, and a couple of phone calls confirmed it beyond doubt.

She sighed and typed the third name that had made her cop senses tingle into the computer, then hit 'search.'

By the time her shift was over, so was her research on Roger Glomes.

Another dead end.

Pete Jenkins was just about to log out for the day when he looked at his computer screen and frowned.

"That can't be right. Maybe I input my search parameters incorrectly," he mumbled under his breath, then reviewed what he'd done.

No, I did it right. What the hell?

Confused, he built his search again from scratch, then left it to run overnight and headed home.

Nathan and Bella stood side-by-side in their kitchen, working to put dinner together.

"How does it feel to officially be done with your master's degree?" he asked with a grin as he pulled the pasta bake out of the oven.

"Surreal," his wife answered with a laugh. "But also awesome, I'm not gonna lie."

She pivoted around him to slide the small tray of garlic bread into the open oven, then closed the door and set the timer.

"I'm just going to go check on Charlie," she said, and kissed his cheek. "I'll be right back."

A few moments later she returned, smiling.

"I think his fever finally broke, and he's sleeping soundly," she announced. "Hopefully he'll be his old cheerful self in the morning."

"He wasn't fussy, really," Nathan informed her. "But it was obvious he wasn't feeling good. He wasn't hungry, and he was happiest when I had him snuggled up in my lap."

"I bet. I know *I'm* happy when I'm snuggled up with you," she said, and received a passionate kiss in return.

When the timer went off, Bella pulled the garlic bread from the oven and helped her husband dish up two plates. They sat at the table next to one another and began to eat.

"So," she said as casually as she could manage, "you've got that look on your face."

"What look?"

"Your *I am frustrated* look. Talk to me, honey. What's going on?"

"It's just this case I've got," he told her. "Very little headway so far, so, you're right, I'm frustrated."

No way in hell I'm telling her that everybody, including my boss, thinks that I'm the real target....

"Just keep working the angles, babe. You'll figure it out. You always do."

He squeezed her hand.

"You know, I *do* have a way to take your mind off of it for a while," she revealed with a sensual smile.

"Soak time?"

"Soak time. But let's finish dinner first, and then..."

"Hi mommy," came a sleep-filled voice from the doorway leading down the hall.

"Hey, sweetie! How are you feeling? Any better?"

Charlie nodded.

"Are you hungry, little man?" Nathan asked.

Charlie nodded again.

"Okay. How about a grilled cheese? And then we'll do bath time and story time," Bella offered.

"Daddy read *Three Little Pigs*?" Charlie asked, his eyes wide with hope.

"Absolutely, buddy," Nathan told him. "Come on, let's get you set up in your chair."

He helped Charlie up into his booster seat then crossed over to where Bella was putting a buttered slice of bread face-down in the frying pan and whispered in her ear.

"Is soak time still on the table?"

"Absolutely. The minute he's asleep again, you're all mine, Agent Thomas," she whispered back.

"Good. I was counting on that," he answered, and kissed her before he rejoined their son at the table.

Over in Dallas, Nelson arrived at seven o'clock on the dot to pick Noelle up for their night out. When she opened her apartment door he was temporarily struck dumb at the sight of her little black dress with the plunging neckline. The form-fitting fabric hugged every voluptuous curve in just the right way and the hemline ended about mid-thigh.

Man, oh man. She's hot. I thought the peek down her shirt was breathtaking but this...

She smiled, a slow, sultry one as she turned in place on her five-inch heels.

"You like?"

"I *definitely* like," he replied, and thought, *no harm mixing a little pleasure with business. I'd say I've earned it.*

"Shall we?"

With a giggle, she closed the distance between them, and they stepped out into the foyer together. She locked her door and tucked the key into the tiny black clutch she carried, then slipped her hand into his.

"Ready when you are," she said in a breathy tone that made him smile.

Oh, darlin. You have no idea what you just signed on for, he purred in his head as he held open the passenger door for her then strolled around to climb behind the wheel.

They went for drinks as planned, then dinner, then dancing, before returning to her place for a nightcap.

By the time he let himself out of her apartment in the wee hours of Thursday morning, he'd left Noelle exhausted and breathless, and they were both thoroughly satisfied.

He'd also secured her solemn promise to make a complete copy of Annie Adams' tenant paperwork to give to him when he returned for a stay-in dinner and movie date at her apartment on Friday night.

Chapter Seventeen

SAM TRAILED Bella Thomas again on Thursday morning, and this time was successful in following her to Charlie's daycare. Once Bella left, Sam drove around the block and parked along the street so that the view to the back door of the daycare was unimpeded before unpacking the needed gear and settling in to wait.

The first phone call came around ten o'clock. Bella had only been home for about fifteen minutes after dropping Charlie off at daycare when the phone in Nathan's home office began to ring. But because it was seldom used unless he was working from home, she frowned in confusion at first.

Once she realized what was making the noise, she quickly added soap to the washer and started it, then headed toward Nathan's office. Even as she moved toward it, she chastised herself for the rush.

I feel like Pavlov's dog... Probably just some random telemarketer anyway. Everyone we know calls our cell phones...

"Hello?" she said, a little out of breath.

No answer.

"Hello?" Bella said again.

After a long silence, the caller disconnected.

"Huh," Bella mused, then shrugged it off and returned to the laundry room to continue sorting clothes.

In Dallas, Nathan had rejoined Lizzie in the conference room.

"Charlie feeling better today?" she asked.

"Yes, he's back to normal. We're not sure what caused him to spike a fever, but he woke up hungry around six o'clock last night. We had dinner and bath and story time, and he went right to sleep as usual."

"How far did you get in the story this time?"

Nathan chuckled. "He stayed awake for the whole thing but was out like a light pretty much right after I said, 'the end'."

"Aww," Lizzie sighed. "I love that little dude so, so much."

"Yeah, he's a pretty cool little guy if I do say so myself. So, made any progress?" he asked, and gestured at the papers Lizzie had spread out across her half of the conference table.

"Some," she admitted. "I was able to rule out three of the people that had my gut tingling. Two of them are dead, one moved overseas."

"Since you've ruled them out, mind sharing who they are?"

"Brady Tavert, Angie Sophir, and Roger Glomes."

"Ah," Nathan said, his eyes alit with memory. "Tavert. I remember him for sure. Sneaky as hell and a mean right cross. He rang my bell *hard*. He was out on bail and wrapped his car around a telephone pole at seventy miles an hour because he was blitzed out of his mind."

He tapped his fingers on the desk.

"What about the other two?"

"Angie moved to Scotland eighteen months ago, and I confirmed she's still there."

"Good for her. I was hoping she'd get her act together. She wasn't a bad person, just running with the wrong crowd. What about Glomes?"

"Well, from what I found on him, he actually got his act together, too," Lizzie told him. "But he was killed during a robbery three years ago. Some sixteen-year-old kid held up the convenience store where Glomes was working the overnight shift. The robber shot and killed him and stole a grand total of ninety-one dollars and thirty-two cents in cash and four cartons of cigarettes."

"They catch the kid?"

"He was tried as an adult and is serving a forty-year sentence with no parole," she confirmed.

Both were silent for a moment.

"Any other names pop for you?"

"Three more so far. I'm running one of them now."

"You ready for lunch? And what's with the face, kid?" Joe asked from the doorway.

"I just... I don't get it," Pete said. "Did you hear about that client that showed up Tuesday and then left in a huff?"

"Madge mentioned that, yes. What about it?"

"Well, the whole thing just struck me as odd, so I asked her to bring me the paperwork and I started doing some digging."

"Okay. And?"

"And according to every search that I've run so far, Sam H. Thannato doesn't exist, Joe."

"*What?*"

"Come see for yourself," Pete prompted, and eased his wheelchair back so his boss could access the terminal.

Joe stepped into place in front of the keyboard and looked at Pete's results.

"That's the damnedest thing I ever saw," Joe grumbled.

"I know. At first I thought maybe I input something wrong. But this is the third time I've run it, and every single time *that* is what I get."

"I wonder..." Joe began.

"You wonder what?"

"You know I told you a couple days ago about Nathan Thomas calling me?"

"Yes. You think this might have been an attempt on your life?"

"I know one way we can try to find out. You still have the papers Thannato filled out?"

"Right there," Pete answered and pointed to a manila file folder on the desk.

Joe grabbed his cell phone and dialed.

"Hey, Nathan, it's Joe. Got something strange going on here. You busy?... Well, we had a client show up here Tuesday morning and act strange when they couldn't meet with me personally. Pete got suspicious and tried to run a background check... Yeah, I know, but here's the thing. The name doesn't show up. *At all.* Not with the Department of Motor Vehicles, not with Social Security, hell, not even with the Internal Revenue Service. It's like this person doesn't exist."

Joe paused and listened.

"Sure, I can do that. I'll let you know. See you later."

He hung up and looked at Pete.

"Nathan suggested that I run these pages up to Trish. Her lab has the notes that were left for him at the McNamara and Patterson crime scenes. He said to ask Trish to compare the handwriting. That should rule this Thannato in or out, and we can go from there."

"Rain check on lunch, then," Pete offered.

"Why don't you come with me?"

Pete waved him off with a grin. "I'm good. We can go tomorrow."

Once Nathan had completed his call with Joe, he looked over at Lizzie.

"I think our mystery guest paid a visit to Joe's office," he said, then relayed the conversation he'd just had with Joe to her.

Lizzie's eyebrows peaked.

"Definitely unusual. They going to run that over to Trish now?"

"I assume so, yes."

"I wonder how long it will take to confirm whether it's the same person who wrote all three?"

Nathan sighed. "I have no idea."

Patience finally paid off a little before one p.m. when a group of small children ran out of the daycare's back door and over to the playground equipment in the middle of the oversized fenced backyard.

Sam got several excellent photographs to work with, even with the chain link fence in the way, thanks to a high-quality long-range camera lens. After the camera equipment was packed away again, Sam smiled before putting the car's transmission into drive and slowly easing away from the curb.

At the lab in downtown Fort Worth, Joe kissed his surprised wife on the cheek.

"Did we schedule lunch and I forgot?" Trish asked.

"Nope, this is an impromptu visit, although I would never turn down a chance to spend time with you, honey. I need you to look at these."

He held out the manila folder, and Trish pulled on latex gloves before she took it from him.

"How many people have touched this?" she asked with a frown.

"Because if you need fingerprints, I'll have to have samples to compare to so I can rule them out."

"Fingerprints might be useful but that's not the main focus," Joe assured her. "Nathan and I talked about this, and he mentioned that you have the two notes that were left for him at those murder scenes."

"I do," she confirmed. "What does that have to do with this paperwork?"

Joe sighed then braced himself.

"Well," he said sheepishly, "we're wondering if the same person filled those out as wrote those notes."

She opened the folder and glanced at the first page.

"This... this is your intake form," she breathed, her eyes darting back up to meet his.

"This person was at your office?"

"Yes. So, it's important to confirm whether the handwriting matches."

"I know that. I'm just a little confused. If it was the same person, why didn't they try to..."

"I didn't meet with them," he elaborated. "I was already booked offsite, so I asked Pete to meet them instead, and when this Thannato character realized they wouldn't be dealing with me directly, they threw a fit and stormed out."

Trish glanced down again and noticed the date on the page.

"This happened on *Tuesday*, and I'm just now hearing about it?" she asked as she narrowed her eyes, set the folder down, and crossed her arms over her chest.

"Now wait a minute, honey," he said, his hands extended in front of him to try to placate her. "We didn't realize something was fishy until about a half-hour ago."

When she raised her eyebrow and held his gaze, Joe explained himself.

"Oh," she said once he was done filling in the gaps. "Okay. Things make more sense now. For a minute there I was worried you'd started keeping things from me."

He closed the distance between them and took her hands in his. "Never, my love."

"Good. And considering what you've told me, I will run a full work up on these pages, including prints, since the name you were given is an obvious fake."

She quickly logged the folder and its contents before she placed it in an evidence bag and carried it over to an open workstation. Then Trish returned to her desk, took off her gloves, opened her desk drawer and pulled out her purse.

"Come on. Let's head to Romano's for a quick lunch. I'm starved, and I have a feeling I'm going to be late for dinner tonight."

By five p.m. the Thomas household had received five more mysterious calls – each of them coming up as 'restricted' on the combination phone and answering machine's display.

The first three Bella had answered, and they'd ranged from deep, heavy breathing but no words spoken to a low, growly, distorted voice whose sentences were almost impossible to understand.

The last two had come in while she'd left the house to go to the post office and grocery store and then to pick Charlie up from daycare. As a result, the answering machine had fielded them.

The two messages that Bella heard when she played them back made the hair at the back of her neck stand up. No direct threats, just different variations of an ominous *'I'll be seeing you soon'*- type message emanating from the tiny speaker in a deep voice that she could tell had been altered somehow.

The real question is, do I tell Nathan? she worried as she unpacked groceries and put them away in her kitchen while an oblivious Charlie watched cartoons in the living room.

I'm sure it's just some kids prank calling, she finally decided. *Nathan's dealing with enough as it is right now. I'm sure this is a one-off deal.*

Having talked herself down, she moved over to the counter by the stove.

"Hey, Charlie. How about tacos for dinner?" she called out.

"Aw! Mac and cheese?" her son responded back, and she laughed.

"Why am I not surprised?"

Above the bookstore, Rick grinned from ear to ear and pumped his fist in the air.

"Yes! I'm in. It's about damn time, too," he crowed as he began to type furiously on his laptop.

"Now to pull some weeds...".

"Huh?" Faith said from behind him. "What the hell, honey?"

"It's okay," Rick answered without looking up as his fingers flew across the keyboard. "I'm helping Nathan with something."

"Oh. Okay," she said and patted his shoulder before she walked away toward the kitchen.

Well, technically I'm helping him with two *somethings, but he'll never know about the second one. No one will. It's called plausible deniability,* Rick acknowledged with a grin as he put the finishing touches on his final commands, then hit 'enter'.

Chapter Eighteen

By mid-morning Friday she'd managed to cross off another name from Nathan's past, and Lizzie set her sights on tracking down the last two that had caught her attention.

She cleared her previous searches, typed in the next to last name she'd found, and pressed 'enter'. Then she stood, stretched, grabbed her empty coffee mug, and headed to the breakroom for a refill.

Nathan was standing in front of the breakroom coffeemaker with his hands on his hips and a scowl on his face.

"Uh oh. Did we run out again?"

"Worse," he growled. "This damn thing quit working."

She paled. "No."

"Yeah," he confirmed, and angrily shoved his hands into his front pockets. "Which sucks."

"Completely. What do we do?"

"No worries," came a voice from the doorway.

They both turned and watched as Diane, their unit secretary, carried in a large box.

"I ordered this late last week when I noticed that thing was acting up. It was time for an upgrade anyway," she said with a smile. "Move that piece of junk out of the way and help me get this unpacked, and I'll set it up."

"Have I told you lately that you rock?" Nathan asked as he took the package from her, set it down on the table, and whipped out his pocketknife to slice through the wide band of tape that secured the top seam of the box.

"No," she quipped, "but then again, I did this for selfish reasons. You two aren't the only ones in this office that run on caffeine, you know."

"Well, if it wasn't official before, it is now. You're our hero, Diane," Lizzie told her with a huge grin.

"Yeah, yeah," Diane kidded back. "Unplug that antique, would you?"

Not ten minutes later, two very happy agents and one very happy unit secretary retreated to their respective work areas with fresh cups of perfectly brewed nectar.

***

From his vantage point down the shoreline, Hank glanced occasionally in the direction of the Adams cabin as he reeled his fishing pole's line in, then cast it out again.

He'd only caught a few glimpses of Annie and her parents since he'd settled into his tiny rental, but those brief fleeting moments had been enough to reassure him that the trio was safe for the time being.

Hank's gaze lingered for a while on the bright orange bobber as it bounced merrily on the water's softly rippling surface. But as the slight breeze he'd been enjoying grew a bit stronger, he tilted his head upward to observe the increasingly overcast sky.

We're gonna have some severe storms coming soon, he acknowledged with a frown. *In more ways than one. I just hope I'm equal to the task.*

Trish Wallace set her magnifying glass down and frowned.

"Dammit."

"What's wrong?" her assistant asked from across the workspace.

"I just can't be sure," Trish admitted as she gestured to the three sets of handwriting she'd been trying to compare.

"These look the same to me, but I'm just not comfortable saying for certain without a *known* document from this individual to compare these to."

"Maybe give Dr. Bailey a call?" her assistant suggested.

Trish nodded. "That was my next step."

She walked to her office, sat at her desk, and dialed the cell phone number for Dr. Agnes Bailey, who was a good friend but who also happened to be one of the country's foremost handwriting analysis experts.

"Good morning, Agnes, it's Trish," she began. "I have some samples that I could really use your opinion on."

By four-thirty that afternoon, Bella had had enough.

The mysterious calls to the Thomas household had continued, and when she finally lost her temper just enough to be rude, the calls increased not just in frequency but in tone and aggressiveness.

She finally opted to turn the house phone's ringer off, and only two things stopped her from dismantling the device completely.

First was the fact that Nathan might get a work-related inbound call – and second, that a sizeable portion of Nathan's large, heavy wooden desk blocked the way to the connections point with the cord running to the wall port.

Nelson pulled in and parked in front of Noelle's building at five minutes to six. But since he'd already planned for tonight's rendezvous to end a completely different way than their previous one had, he made sure to activate the jammer signal this time before leaving his Land Rover and strolling up to her door.

"Perfect timing," Noelle announced when she opened the door. "I just drained the pasta. Want some wine?"

He held up the bottle he'd brought along.

"Yes, and I'll pour."

He trailed behind her into the apartment, taking care not to use his hand, but his elbow to close the door behind them.

Nelson followed her into her small kitchen and sniffed the air.

"That smells really good," he observed. "What is it we're having?"

"Shrimp piccata with angel hair pasta," Noelle replied with a smile as she plated two generous portions, then topped each with fresh parsley. "And I think the oven timer's just about to go off. Can you pull the bread out of there, please?"

"Happy to."

He deftly removed the long, narrow baking sheet and set it down on the counter where she had two trivets waiting.

"Okay. We need the bread and butter on the table, and we're ready to eat," Noelle said with a smile as she carried the two plates over to her dinette table.

"And the wine," he pointed out. "Where's your corkscrew?"

"Third drawer to the left," she answered as she cut the freshly baked bread into thick slices, placed them in a towel-covered bowl, then retrieved the butter from the fridge and set both items on the table.

Meanwhile, Nelson worked the cork carefully from the bottle of chardonnay, poured wine into two glasses, and carried them across to the table.

They sat across from each other, and Nelson raised his glass in a toast.

"To an unforgettable evening," he proclaimed, and Noelle giggled.

"Hear, hear," she replied as they clinked their glasses together.

He waited until they were midway through the delicious meal that she'd prepared before he asked her the single question he really needed an answer to.

"So, did you manage to get that file copied for me?"

"I did," she confirmed with a smile. "But it wasn't easy, and I almost got caught, so, you owe me big time, darlin.'"

Yes... This means I can forge ahead as planned...

"I told you I'd make it worth your while," he said with a suggestive smile.

She giggled again.

"Good, because I intend to collect," she told him. "Beginning with you staying the night."

Nelson gazed at her across the table and told his first lie of the evening.

"I'd already planned to."

Meanwhile, Pete Jenkins was like a bulldog with a bone.

He'd readily handed over the pages that the mysterious Sam H. Thannato had written on. But the fact that the name appeared exactly nowhere in any database at all had stuck in his craw, making him crazy with a deep-seated need to solve the puzzle.

Pete's growing obsession had resulted in a very sleepless Thursday night, and Friday night wasn't looking promising, either.

"Maybe it's encrypted or something?" he mused aloud after he'd considered then discarded other theories.

He grabbed a fresh legal pad from his desk drawer and set it down in the middle of his blotter, then carefully wrote out 'Sam H. Thannato' in block letters.

"Old school trial and error, I guess," he muttered as he began to play around with various letter combinations.

Twenty minutes later he was dialing Joe's cell phone number.

"I figured it out," he exclaimed the moment Joe picked up the call. "It's an anagram."

"Woah, kid. Slow down. What are you talking about?"

"Sam H. Thannato. If you rearrange the letters, you get Nathan Thomas."

Silence.

"Joe?"

"Yeah, I'm here. Good work, Pete. I'll call Nathan now."

———

Later, after he'd insisted on helping her with the dishes, Noelle threw Nelson a coquettish look.

"How about you pour us some more wine while I go put on something more... comfortable?'

He grinned. "Absolutely. Shall I wait out here?"

"If you like. I'll just be a moment."

Nelson watched her saunter away, her full, lush curves swaying, taunting him with every step. Once she'd disappeared down the hall, he slipped a hand into his jacket pocket. He removed the tiny vial he'd brought along and tipped its contents into Noelle's wineglass. The vial was quickly returned to his pocket, and he finished off with more wine in each long-stemmed glass.

Then he moved to the living room, where the eight-by-eleven manila envelope that bore his name – '*Dylan*', the fake name he'd used on his process server nametag – was lying on her coffee table in front of her leather couch. He set the wine down, picked up the envelope, opened it, and quickly scanned the first page contained inside. What he saw had him smiling from ear to ear, and he refastened the tiny copper brads to close the envelope again, then returned it to its original place on the table.

Within five minutes, Noelle reappeared in his line of sight, wearing a red satin robe – and not much else.

He crossed the space between them slowly, one wineglass in each hand, and offered Noelle hers.

"Another toast is in order, I believe. To us," he murmured.

"To us," she parroted, and never broke eye contact with him as she took a long, long drink.

When her glass was empty, she set it down on the closest flat surface, then held out her hand.

"Time to collect," she purred.

Nelson responded by setting his own half-full glass down, sweeping her up into his arms, and carrying her to the bedroom. He set her down gently and began to kiss her, gradually turning up the intensity as he went.

Three minutes in, he realized that the heavy tranquilizer he'd slipped her had begun to take effect. Noelle's head lolled back, and her speech began to slur.

"There, there, darling. Lie back," he softly whispered, and she made a strange little mewling sound as she obeyed.

"Don't... feel right..." she mumbled.

"I know, Noelle. Here's the thing," he said as he removed his suit jacket and tossed it over a chair, then climbed up onto the bed on his knees beside her.

"You're a great woman. You're beautiful and captivating and I could spend years enjoying every single inch of you," he said as he took off his necktie.

She peered up at him through heavy-lidded eyes and opened her mouth to speak, but he leaned down and used a passionate kiss as a distraction while he worked his tie underneath and around her neck, then crisscrossed the ends at the front of her throat.

"There's only one problem," he whispered against her panting mouth when he broke the kiss. "You can't keep a secret to save your life. Literally."

With that, he sat upright and swung his right leg over so that he was straddling her torso, gripped each end of his tie tightly in his fists, and pulled as hard as he could.

Noelle struggled, but it was in vain; he'd taken care to pin her arms to her sides underneath his muscled frame as he'd moved above her. Her eyes bulged as he maintained lethal tension around her throat, and her body bucked underneath him as her fight to live raged on.

At long last, she went limp and still, and Nelson released his grip on his neckwear only long enough to check her carotid for a pulse. As he suspected, there wasn't one.

The shocked, accusing, drug-hazed stare skyward of her open eyes caused one single sharp pang of regret. Nelson reached down and gently lowered her eyelids, then closed his own eyes and allowed himself to wallow in what might have been for the space of a handful of moments before he shrugged it off.

Once he'd climbed off her, he smoothed down her robe and worked the necktie that he'd dug deeply into her soft flesh loose again. Then he put his jacket back on, tucked his tie into a pocket, and retreated to the living room.

He pulled on the latex gloves he'd stashed in his inside jacket pocket, then placed both wineglasses and the metal corkscrew he'd touched bare-handed in the top rack of the dishwasher. Once he'd confirmed that everything else he'd touched had already been loaded he started the machine.

After that, he wiped down and threw away the empty wine bottle he'd brought with him, then walked over to the coffee table and triumphantly picked up the envelope that held the keys to finally tracking down Annie Adams.

Nelson checked his jammer signal to ensure it was still turned on before he opened Noelle's front door a crack and peeked outside. Seeing no one in the vicinity, he stepped out and closed the door softly behind him, then strode quickly to his Land Rover.

It wasn't until he was behind the wheel with his doors locked and his engine running that he took off the gloves and turned off the signal jammer.

He pulled out of the parking spot and left the complex, whistling gaily as he went along.

Over in Pantego, Nathan crept out of Charlie's room and shut the door behind him.

"He's out. Race you to the tub," he told Bella, who smiled.

"That sounds like heaven," she answered, then pretended to turn to go to the living room before darting around him and scampering down the hallway and into their master bedroom with her arms raised over her head to signal victory.

He chuckled to himself as he followed her.

She ran the water and added an essential oil, and as they both undressed she looked at him and asked, "You okay, babe? Making any headway on your case?"

He paused, still unwilling to confess to her that he had more than one target painted on his back – and that one of the people hunting him was using a fictitious name based on his.

Creepy as hell. Still can't quite believe that, he admitted, recalling the revealing talk he'd had with Joe on his drive home.

"Babe?"

"Not really," he finally answered.

"You will. I believe in you," she said simply as she climbed into the garden tub and held her arms out to him. "Now, come join me."

Nathan smiled and did exactly as she asked.

When Nelson arrived back at Ramon's place, he sat down at his laptop then opened the envelope and pulled out the six pages of data that Noelle had copied for him.

"Interesting," he murmured when he noticed the emergency contact section of Annie's rental application. Although the address was blank, there was a name and a phone number listed – a John and Mary Adams.

Nelson cross-checked the phone prefix on his web browser.

"Northeastern Oklahoma," he noted. "Let's see how many John Adams there are in that area."

He built his search, hit enter, then stood to go change out of his suit. By the time he returned, clad in sweatpants and a t-shirt, the results were in.

"*Seven?* Seriously?"

Nelson sighed, then shrugged his shoulders and began to write down all the addresses showing in his search results.

Guess I'm spending quality time in northeastern Oklahoma this weekend...

It was almost nine p.m. when Nelson finished packing up his gear and hauled it out to the Land Rover. He drove to the gas station down the street and inserted the cartel-provided debit card into the pump's card reader, then keyed in his PIN number.

He did a double-take when the pump's display read *Card Declined.*

"O...kay," he muttered in confusion and withdrew that card, then tried his personal one and got the same result.

Irritated, he walked into the store.

"Sorry, man, our card readers are acting up again," the clerk explained.

Nelson paid for fifty dollars' worth of gas with cash, then returned outside and operated the pump. That accomplished, he climbed back behind the wheel, set his GPS coordinates for the first address on his list, and navigated to the highway to head north.

A little over four hours later, he arrived on the outskirts of Tulsa, Oklahoma, and paid cash for a nondescript room in a nondescript motel. While the exterior of the place didn't look like much, he was pleasantly surprised that the room itself was very clean and comfortable. He set an alarm for six a.m., then drifted off to sleep.

Chapter Nineteen

"Wʜᴀᴛ's ᴜᴘ?" Hank said when he answered Nathan's call a little before nine on Saturday morning.

"Quite a bit, actually," the agent replied. "I just got word that there were confirmed sightings of Nelson's Land Rover heading north on Interstate 75 through Dallas."

"When?"

"Last night around ten. Dallas PD's reaching out to each city along that route to try and pinpoint exactly where he went, but they haven't gotten any feedback yet."

"Thanks for the heads up. Sounds like our wait might be over before too much longer."

"Just be damn careful - and keep me updated."

"Yes, papa," Hank quipped and made Nathan chuckle before he hung up the phone.

By nine-thirty a frustrated Nelson was climbing back into his Land Rover in Broken Arrow, Oklahoma.

Grumbling under his breath, he crossed out the third address on his list, then programmed his GPS to guide him to the fourth one located on the northwest side of Tulsa.

"Thank God there's only seven to check out," he muttered to himself as he fastened his seat belt and pulled away from the curb.

He took a deep breath and willed himself to be patient for the twenty-two-mile drive.

I've come this far. I just have to keep going.

An hour after he left Broken Arrow, Nelson struck paydirt.

Addresses four and five had been a bust, and his already simmering temper crept towards boiling over by the time he pulled into an older, well-maintained neighborhood in Tulsa's Riverview Historic District.

He maneuvered his Land Rover to the curb and parked in front of the sixth address on his list, a two-story craftsman-style home with a beautifully landscaped yard.

Nelson climbed out of his vehicle and stepped onto the side-walk. But before he could approach the house, someone called out to him.

"Morning!" came a cheerful, chirpy voice from his left.

He turned his head to see who'd greeted him. It was an older woman dressed in loose, flowing clothing. A wide-brimmed, floppy hat obscured the top part of her face from view, but he noticed a small trowel in her hand.

"Morning," he replied politely. "Getting some gardening done?"

"Yep, before it gets too hot," she confirmed with a chuckle. "Only supposed to get to eighty degrees today but even that's too much for me if it's humid out. You looking for Annie?"

Nelson's heart skipped a beat, but he kept his tone level and even when he answered, "Why, yes. How did you know?"

"When a handsome young man like you shows up here, it must

be about Annie. You'd make a cute couple," the neighbor said with a mischievous grin.

Her next words made his heart skip again.

"Too bad you missed 'em. I'm not sure how long they're gonna be down there."

"Beg pardon?"

"They headed to their lake house, honey. Mary asked me to collect their mail while they're gone."

Nelson scrambled to produce a convincing lie.

"Aw, man, I missed it," he proclaimed, and tried his best to sound forlorn. "I promised Annie I'd go but I got hung up with work and didn't get to leave Dallas until this morning."

He looked at her and poured on the charm.

"And I don't know where the lake house is. I've tried calling Annie several times, but I guess cell phone reception isn't very good out there because I can't get through."

The woman closed the distance and patted his arm.

"No worries, honey. I can give you the address. And you'll love it out there, it's beautiful. Nice and quiet, too. Great place to get away and just relax."

She turned and headed toward her front door.

"I'll be right back," she called out over her shoulder.

Nelson stood on the sidewalk, stunned but pleased at the woman's helpfulness – and chattiness – to a total stranger.

Thanks, lady. You just saved me some time.

For a moment, he contemplated following her into her home and killing her once she'd given him the address, then decided against it. *No real need. She doesn't know my name or anything about me, and by the time she hears Annie's dead I'll be long gone.*

Satisfied that his decision to spare her was the right one, he waited patiently for her return. A few more minutes passed, and she reappeared in front of him and held out a small, sky-blue scrap of paper.

"Sorry it took me so long," she said with an embarrassed smile. "I keep misplacing my notepad and pen. Had to search for them."

"No problem. I really appreciate the help. Thank you so much," he said with a genuine smile back and a nod.

"You're very welcome. Have fun!" she replied, beaming, then turned her attention back to the flowerbed she'd been working in when he arrived.

He slid behind the wheel and started the engine, then programmed the new destination into his GPS and whistled when the results displayed onscreen.

"Three-hour ride, huh," he observed, then glanced at his fuel gauge. "Better fill up first."

With a last wave to the friendly old lady, Nelson smoothly pulled away from the curb to search for the closest gas station.

He turned into a lot and parked next to a gas pump, then stepped out to use his company card.

Declined.

"Seriously?"

He tried his personal card next, and it worked fine.

That's odd, he thought to himself as he filled his tank.

When he was done he hung up the hose, twisted the gas cap back into position, and climbed back behind the wheel.

He started the vehicle, then pressed the button on the steering wheel to activate the Land Rover's hands-free calling feature.

Nelson spoke a name as he strapped on his seat belt.

"It's me," he said when the other party answered. "Checking in. Everything okay there?"

He listened, frowning, as the person he was talking to fed him what felt like a massive lie.

"Should I come back?" Nelson asked, then waited.

"Okay, then. I'll call you when it's done."

He pressed the disconnect button to end the call and frowned at his reflection in his rear-view mirror as he put the Rover into gear.

Something big is happening down there. The question is, what?

"Later," he chided his mirror image. "Focus."

One quick glance at the GPS screen to get his bearings, and Nelson's three-hour trip south got underway.

He'd been on the road for an hour when his stomach grumbled, and Nelson opted to stop in the next small town he came to – Prague, Oklahoma.

He found a family-style diner with plenty of open seating, and the hostess guided him to a booth along the far wall. After he'd given the waitress his order, he removed his laptop from its carrying bag and fired it up.

He navigated to Google Maps and entered in the address that the Adams' neighbor had so thoughtfully provided, then switched to satellite view.

"Huh. Tishomingo," he noted as he jotted down the lake house's exact coordinates, then turned his attention to Tishomingo National Wildlife Refuge.

Nelson opened a new browser window to learn more about the refuge and was pleasantly surprised to find out that overnight camping was allowed.

Next, he pulled up a map of the refuge and calculated the distance from the closest camping area within the refuge to the edge of the Adams property.

Five and a half miles. Piece of cake. I can hike that in my sleep.

He paused his activity and moved his laptop to the side as his meal arrived.

"Excuse me, miss," Nelson said as his waitress set his plate down in front of him. "Is there any place in town to buy camping gear?"

End of Secrets

By four p.m. the gray Land Rover had turned right onto Refuge Road and followed the winding pavement another three miles until the visitor's center of Tishomingo National Wildlife Refuge came into view.

Nelson parked, then casually strolled inside.

"Afternoon," he said with his most charming smile to the lady at the counter. "Any camping spots open?"

"We have a few left," she confirmed. "How many nights?"

"Two, please," he replied, and pulled out his wallet.

A few minutes later she handed him a receipt, a temporary windshield decal, and a map of the refuge that showed its entire layout.

"Your site's down here," she said, and pointed to a campground area labeled Lost Lake.

Yes, he gloated in his head. *Right where I wanted to be.*

"Thanks."

"You're welcome. Enjoy your stay."

If you only knew, Nelson thought as he smiled and turned to go back out to his vehicle.

Within fifteen minutes he'd pulled into the much smaller lot in the Lost Lake campground. Nelson retrieved the one-person hiker tent he'd bought and set it up in camping slot number seven, then retreated to his Land Rover to check his current position against the latitude and longitude of the family summer retreat where Annie and her parents had gone into hiding.

"Yep, just about five and a half miles, give or take," he murmured, then looked through the windshield at his surroundings.

While the terrain was flat as far as he could see, it was also overgrown. Lush, dense foliage seemed to be a staple of the refuge's natural features, only broken up by narrow walking trails strewn here and there.

But I am definitely not going to be staying on the path, he conceded with a grin, then returned his focus to plotting out the course he would take after dark.

Once Nelson was satisfied with the chosen route, he exited the vehicle again to place his duffel bag and sleeping bag inside his tent.

Better get some sleep, he decided. *It's game on come nightfall.*

Years of discipline and training enabled him to drift off quickly after he set his watch's alarm for midnight.

A scream jolted him awake just after ten p.m.

"What the hell?" Nelson muttered as he bolted upright, pulse quickening, and strained to listen.

It sounded again, and he grinned.

Bobcat, he realized. *Guess there are other animals here besides a bunch of birds after all.*

He checked his watch and nodded.

Close enough.

Nelson kept his movements small and efficient within the confines of the tent and used a penlight to retrieve what he needed from the duffel bag for his overnight excursion.

He changed clothes quickly – black combat fatigues and boots, then strapped one knife to his thigh and set another at his waist, along with his HK45. The last piece he added to his ensemble was his night-vision goggles; these he slung around his neck by the strap.

Next, he took a few minutes to wolf down an energy bar and program the lake house coordinates into his smartwatch as he listened to his surroundings. No sounds emanated from any of the other campsites.

Satisfied, Nelson crept out of his tent, then crouched down beside it in the pitch black of a cloud-covered night and waited another two minutes to be certain no one else in the area was awake.

He raised his left arm and tapped the watch's face to pull up the display, oriented himself, fitted his goggles over his eyes, and began his trek southeast.

Chapter Twenty

By MIDNIGHT, Nelson was grateful that the screaming bobcat had kicked off his journey two hours earlier than planned. The route he'd plotted to his destination was much thicker with overgrowth than he'd anticipated. As a result, his top speed was averaging one mile per hour rather than the three miles per hour he had been counting on.

What I wouldn't give for a machete, he grumbled to himself as he struggled to cut through another tangle of vines. Both knives he carried were designed for combat and ill-suited to hacking through such dense underbrush.

Nelson's blade finally severed the last stubborn tendril, and he was relieved to find his feet on one of the narrow dirt trails that ran through the refuge.

Change of plans, he decided as he took in his surroundings, then lifted his goggles, retrieved the park's map from his pocket, and shined his penlight on its surface.

Ah. There. Time to take a more direct route. Higher risk of being spotted, but anything's better than this...

A few taps on his smartwatch reset his GPS to return him to the campground, and he began to jog that direction.

The solemn *ping, ping* coming from his smartwatch had Hank Myers sitting upright, then flinging the covers back at two-twenty-two a.m.

He launched himself across the space toward his laptop to confirm what his gut instinct suspected – that two of his sensors had captured movement that wasn't of the animal variety.

Hank tapped a few keys to pinpoint those sensors' locations, scanned the recording, and calculated in his head.

Ten minutes, twelve at the most.

He hurriedly pulled on black clothing and his Kevlar vest, grabbed his gun, knife, and goggles, then raced out the door and down the dock to the boat.

Hank slipped on his goggles, then cast off and used the trolling motor to turn the boat around then point it toward the cabin where Annie was staying.

The journey from dock to dock took just over two minutes, and Hank was grateful that his temporary landlord had invested in quality gear – the motor was so quiet that the only evidence of a boat moving through the water at all were the ripples left in its wake.

He maneuvered to the dock behind Annie's cabin, tied off the boat, then stepped out onto the dock and glanced down at his smart-watch just as it pinged again.

The third sensor's position confirmed the trajectory Nelson was taking – and that he'd arrive in front of the cabin in roughly three more minutes.

Hank crept forward from the end of the dock onto land, then stealthily made his way to the southwestern corner of the cabin where he could see Nelson's approach and settled in with his gun at the ready.

A fourth soft ping alerted him that Nelson would be coming into view within the next ninety seconds.

Showtime.

Inside the cabin, a yawning Annie stumbled out of the bathroom and made her way back down the dark hall to her room in the southwest corner of the cabin. She was about to crawl back into bed when she heard an unfamiliar sound, soft but clear, coming from outside her window.

She crept over to the window and glanced out, first left, then right, and was shocked to see the back of someone's head barely visible in the deep shadows.

Shit. He found me!

She whirled and went to her dresser to retrieve her service weapon from its holster, then back to her window to look down again at the stranger crouched down outside just as the moon finally broke through the clouds.

Now that the landscape was partially bathed in moonlight, she could see that the figure had a weapon but was pointing it at the trees running along the northwest side of the yard, not at the cabin. She also noticed blond hair, and when the figure lowered his goggles and turned slightly, she saw his profile. Her pulse sped up.

Hank!

Annie hurried back down the hallway to the living room and risked a glance through that window to try to figure out what Hank was so focused on. What she saw almost stopped her in her tracks - another figure dressed head to toe in black was creeping forward from between the trees, gun pointed at the cabin.

She watched, shielding herself from view as much as possible, as the intruder from the trees moved halfway across the open space. Once the figure got close enough that she could confirm that goggles covered the person's eyes, her lip twitched.

Night-vision, huh? Try this on, buddy.

Her service weapon at the ready, Annie reached out to her left and placed her hand on a wall switch, then calmly counted down from ten as the shadow that had emerged from the trees came into range of the powerful twin floodlights that her father had installed over the front door.

Hank tensed as Nelson got within twelve feet of the front steps – and then all hell broke loose. Hank couldn't help but grin as the entire front yard suddenly looked like it was broad daylight rather than not quite three in the morning.

Guess Annie's awake after all, he thought as he watched Nelson curse and stumble, then tear his goggles away from his eyes and blink rapidly.

It was the opening Hank needed, and he promptly sighted in and fired, striking his former teammate three times in the chest, throwing him backward to land hard on the gravel driveway.

Hank quickly closed the distance and kicked away Nelson's gun, but Nelson, who was also wearing a Kevlar vest, drew the knife from the scabbard at his waist and buried it up to the hilt in Hank's outer left thigh.

Hank grimaced and stumbled backward, favoring his left leg. Nelson sprang to his feet, knocked Hank's gun away, and threw two punches that had Hank seeing stars, then dove for his own pistol.

His hand clenched around the grip, and he lurched to his feet again and whipped around to face Hank.

"Guess I win this time," Nelson sneered, and raised his gun to fire.

But another shot echoed through the still night air, and Hank watched, dazed, as Nelson toppled over sideways, dead from a gunshot wound to the left temple.

Stunned, Hank slumped to the soft grass and swiveled his head to the right just in time to see Annie come out of her modified Weaver stance, step down off the porch and hurry over to him.

"Call an ambulance, Dad!" she cried out over her shoulder, which brought Hank's attention to the older man who lowered the double-barreled shotgun he was holding and retreated into the cabin to summon help.

"Hey, you," Annie said softly to Hank as she kneeled beside him and pulled off her terrycloth bathrobe's belt to use as a tourniquet on his leg.

"Hey, tiny. Nice shooting," Hank told her.

"Thanks. How did you find me?"

"Nathan had the guys put a tracker on your loaner car."

She considered that piece of data as she threaded her belt around his upper leg.

"Is that why you got all weird and then went radio dark? To hunt down Nelson?"

"Yes. And I'm sorry if I came across as a jerk, tiny. It was the best way for me to disappear so I could track him."

She wrinkled her nose at him.

"You could have just told me, you know," she said, and pulled the terrycloth belt a little extra tight to prove her point.

Hank winced at both her words and her actions.

"I know, and I'm sorry. But at the time I thought it would be safer for you if I cut all ties."

"Why is that?"

Hank gazed into her eyes and started to answer but her father interrupted them.

"Your mom already called it in, Annie-bug. Ambulance and police are on the way. I'm going down to unlock the gate and lead them in," John Adams announced to them both as he walked to his truck.

They watched him get behind the wheel and back up his truck, then turn and head down the long driveway. Once her dad was out of sight, Annie turned her attention back to the man lying before her on the grass.

"Annie-bug?" Hank asked with a twinkle in his eyes, then grimaced as she tightened the belt further.

"Long story, and you're not answering my question. So, why did you think I'd be safer if you started being a jerk to me?"

"So that he couldn't use you as leverage."

Annie's left eyebrow raised in confusion. "Huh?"

In response, Hank sat up, gently curled his right hand around the nape of her neck and pulled her down into a kiss.

Almost a minute passed before she pulled away, then thumbed over her shoulder at the approaching sirens.

"Um, *wow*. Okay. While they're tending to you I need to call Nathan and let him know we got Nelson."

She paused, then stood up and looked down at him.

"You *do* know that we're going to need to talk later about what just happened here, right?" she admonished.

Hank grinned as he laid flat again, raised his arms, and laced his fingers together to rest his head on them. Except for the knife still protruding from his leg, he felt wonderful - and for the first time in a long time, hopeful.

"Anything you want, tiny. Anything you want."

Chapter Twenty-One

Nathan Thomas eased out of bed a little after seven a.m. so that he would not wake a still sleeping Bella. He slipped on jeans and a t-shirt before he moved quietly down the hall to check on their son.

Charlie had once again kicked his comforter off the bed and onto the floor, and the toddler's outstretched arms and legs were covered in goosepimples even as he slept soundly.

Nathan grinned as he retrieved the comforter from its resting place and lovingly covered Charlie up again, chuckling softly when his child sighed deeply and curled up into a ball. Then he softly shut Charlie's bedroom door and made his way to the kitchen.

A few minutes later Nathan had settled into his home office with the first of several cups of coffee. After a few sips to help clear the slight remnant of cobwebs from his brain that had resulted from a mere four hours of sleep, he opted to start with emails.

The first twelve were routine. The thirteenth, however, stole his breath away and made his pulse pound with white-hot anger.

Its contents were sparse – one sentence, and one image – but designed for maximum impact.

Give yourself up and he won't be hurt.

That sentence was worrisome enough. But it was the single picture the sender had included that made Nathan's blood boil.

The image was of Charlie – head thrown back with laughter – as he played on one of the swings at his daycare's playground.

Nathan stared, shaking with rage, at the single line of words positioned above the picture prominently featured in the email for several moments, then scrambled to get Rick Conner on the phone.

"Hey, I need an urgent trace," he said the moment a sleepy-sounding Rick picked up the call.

"What's going on?"

"Remote into my home computer and you'll see."

"Hang tight."

Three minutes later he knew Rick had connected into his screen and its contents; Rick was controlling the cursor's movements, and when he spoke again his voice was sharp, all traces of sleep gone.

"*Wow.* That's not cool at all..."

"Definitely not. Can you track where this came from?"

"Already working on it. Do not do anything with this, okay? Leave everything right where it is. I'll let you know what I find out."

"Thanks. I appreciate it. And hey, let's keep this between us for now, all right?" Nathan said. "No need to make anyone else worried at the moment, when this could just be some sort of prank."

The brief but poignant pause before Rick answered him made Nathan realize the fallacy of his statement – and that whoever sent the message was deadly serious.

"You and I both know better than that. But yeah, I'll keep this to myself until we can confirm its origin. I'll be in touch," Rick told him grimly, and hung up.

"Come on, man, get me a lead," Nathan muttered as he watched the pointer zip across the screen and thought *they come anywhere near my child again and I will hunt down and kill every last one of them.*

Rick worked on tracing the origins of the ominous email on Nathan's computer. A half-hour later, his suspicions were confirmed, and he reached for the phone to call Nathan back.

"The same person visited Donny's site and Joe's site and sent you that email," he explained the minute Nathan picked up the phone. "It's the same IP address used for all three. I'm starting the trace back to their physical location now."

"How long?"

"Depends on if they were smart enough to bounce it around or not," Rick said. "Could be a few minutes or a few hours. I'll call you back once I have their location, all right?"

"Okay. Thanks, Rick."

As instructed, Nathan left his home office unit alone while Rick worked his magic. He happened to glance over at the answering machine and noticed the red blinking light, so he pressed 'play'.

You have twenty-nine new messages and two old messages, the robotic voice announced, and Nathan's eyebrows shot skyward. Intrigued, he grabbed a clean legal pad and a pen, then followed the prompts to begin listening to them all.

Motion in his periphery caused him to look up and see a pale, trembling Bella standing in the doorway as the first new message played.

"What the hell?" Nathan growled, and played it again, then selected the envelope information so he could capture the date and time it was left on the machine. Then he backed up to the main menu and repeated his efforts with the two old messages.

Dumbfounded, he looked at Bella again and saw guilt etched across her face.

"We've had threatening phone calls coming into this house, and you didn't tell me?" he thundered, his face twisted in anger.

Her shoulders slumped.

"They aren't the first ones," she confessed. "Three before that on Thursday that I answered. Whoever it was kept calling while I went to get Charlie. Then Friday I didn't even bother answering, and I finally just turned the ringer off."

"Someone's been calling here since Thursday morning?"

"Yes."

Nathan pinched the bridge of his nose to try to collect his temper before he spoke again.

"Why didn't you tell me?"

"Because you're dealing with enough right now," she snapped. "And it's probably just some bored high school kid with nothing better to do."

Glaring at her, he pressed 'play' and pointed to the machine as another menacing message filled the air between them.

"You hear that? The voice is distorted on purpose. That's not some kid playing a joke. That's a real threat."

She closed the distance between them and noticed the picture of Charlie on his monitor.

"What.... what is *that?*"

"Someone took a picture of our son at daycare and sent it to me," Nathan muttered, then scrubbed his hands over his face.

She folded her arms over her chest and mirrored his scowl.

"And when was that sent?"

"Sometime last night," he confirmed. "I saw it about an hour ago and asked Rick to investigate it. It's probably part...".

He thought he stopped himself in time, but Bella caught what he said and called him on it.

"Part of what?"

He sighed.

"Someone's targeting me. Both Theresa McNamara and Benji Patterson's bodies had notes left on them that were addressed to me personally."

"*What?* Wait... so you're telling me that in addition to all the stuff going on with the cartel, you've known for over a week that someone else is *also* after you? And yet you've got the nerve to yell at *me* about keeping secrets?"

"Yes. Sort of. I don't know for sure if it's another person altogether, or the cartel working things from two angles," he admitted softly as his temper deflated.

He rose, walked over to her, and wrapped his arms around her.

"I'm sorry I yelled. I was trying to shield you, and I know you were doing the same for me."

She clung to him and rested her forehead on his chest.

"That picture," she croaked. "That's a brand-new shirt Charlie was wearing Thursday – and he spilled grape juice on it after we got home so I put a clean one on him. That means that somebody followed us when I took him to daycare Thursday morning."

She lifted her head and Nathan wiped the tears that streaked down her face.

"If anything happened to him or to you I don't know what I'd..." Bella said on a hard sob.

"I know, baby. I feel the same way."

Nathan's cell phone ringing interrupted.

"Thomas," he growled.

"Found it," he heard Rick say. "A hotel just off Interstate 20 in Arlington. I'm texting you an address now."

"Something else has happened. Evidently we've been getting a series of threatening calls here. Number comes up 'restricted'. Anything you can do with that?"

"Faith and I can be there in the next half-hour, and I'll dig into it when I get there."

"Thanks, man. Appreciate it."

He hung up and looked at Bella.

"They'll be here around eight-thirty. Rick got a lock on where Thannato's been staying. Not that the name means much. Pete Jenkins figured out that it's an anagram of *my* name."

"You need to read me in on this – on *all* of it," she urged as she wiped her cheeks. "No more secrets. Let's go make breakfast and talk."

Lizzie woke suddenly and sat bolt upright in bed.

"What's wrong?" Donny asked on a yawn.

"I have this overwhelming feeling that I really need to run that last name as soon as possible. It can't keep until Monday," she said, then rubbed her eyes and threw back the covers. "I'm going to the office."

"Go shower. I'll make you breakfast and some coffee to take with you," Donny told her, then yawned again.

She was halfway to the bathroom when her cell phone rang from her bedside table. Lizzie pivoted and marched back over to answer it.

"Morning, Nathan. What's up?"

She listened for a few moments, then exclaimed, "You got *what?*" in a deep growl that garnered Donny's full attention.

After a few more minutes passed she said, "Yeah, I'll meet you up there."

"What was that about?" Donny asked her when she set her phone down again.

"Among other things, someone sent Nathan an email with a picture of Charlie in it," she snarled as she paced. "They're targeting that sweet little boy to try to get Nathan to come out and play. But Rick figured out a location, and we're going to go raid it as soon as we're assembled. Nathan's lining out a team. We're meeting at the office in an hour."

She swiveled to face her husband, and he could plainly see fear mixed with fury in her expression.

"And if anyone touches one hair on that precious child's head I will personally send them to Hell."

He scrambled out of bed.

"Go get ready, honey," he urged her. "I'll make a travel mug up for you."

She gathered up clean undergarments, jeans, socks, and a t-shirt and headed for the shower as Donny made a beeline for the kitchen.

Not even fifteen minutes later she'd dried off, dressed, pulled her still damp hair up into a bun, and was sitting on the couch putting on her socks and boots.

True to his word, Donny greeted her in the kitchen doorway with a full travel mug – and a wrapped sandwich for her to take along as well.

"Thanks, baby," she said as she stood and shrugged on her holster, then secured her weapon.

Lizzie walked over to Donny and kissed him then took the food and beverage he'd made for her.

"You be damn careful – and go kick some major ass," he said, and she smiled a hunter's smile.

"Count on it."

From a carefully selected vantage point down the street Sam watched as a truck pulled into the driveway of the Thomas household.

"Interesting," Sam murmured as the vehicle's two occupants got out and walked up to the door. "Wonder who they are?"

Nathan and Rick talked quietly as Rick fired up a laptop he'd brought with him to start his analysis of the inbound calls.

"I talked to my bosses a while ago," Nathan confided to his brother-in-law. "The director's working on a warrant. And Steve's willing to fly down and escort Bella and Charlie back to headquarters if needed, and said he'd guard them personally while they're up in D.C. – but the earliest he can get down here is around noon. Not to mention that every other agent besides Lizzie that I would personally trust to drive them over to meet the plane is out of state, dead, or in hiding right now. I can't put Lizzie on it; she's on the danger list, too."

He paused and ran a hand through his hair.

"But whoever sent that email *also* knows which daycare Charlie attends – and the only way anyone would know that is if Bella was followed, which means whoever this is knows where we live. Which means I don't even know how much longer our home is safe. We could be under surveillance right now for all I know. My gut says send them up to Steve as soon as possible. But at the same time, if they're out in the open...".

"They're more vulnerable," Rick finished. "I get it. Why don't we do this. At this moment it sounds like they are safest staying right here. Faith can keep them company while you, Lizzie, and I go check out that address with your raid team – you might need me there if there's electronics to pick through. If everything goes well, you'll make an arrest onsite. And if not, you and I will escort them to the plane. Okay?"

"Fair enough."

Rick tapped a few keys, then announced, "Okay, I've got the analysis running. Let's head to your office to meet up with your team."

Nathan couldn't help himself.

"Exactly how many computers *do* you own, anyway?"

Rick shrugged his shoulders and grinned.

"I'm afraid that's classified."

Chapter Twenty-Two

Lizzie exited the elevator on the eighth floor and headed straight for the conference room. Her self-assigned mission before other raid team members arrived was to set up the search for the final name on her list.

Once it was underway, she unwrapped the sandwich Donny had made for her and nibbled at it while she gazed at her laptop and willed her machine to go faster.

"Come on, come on. I know I'm not wrong about this," she muttered under her breath. "I can *feel* it."

Several minutes passed before a soft 'ping' sounded, and she grabbed the mouse and maneuvered it to drill down into the records that her search had returned.

"Holy shit," was all she could say at first as her eyes scanned the first five paragraphs of the first record.

Bingo.

She set her sandwich down so that she could use both hands and typed rapidly, then hit the print button to send her first set of data to the big printer down the hall.

Lizzie opened each subsequent record set as they arrived and repeated the process to send each batch to the printer. When she was done she hustled to the copy room to retrieve her documents and carried them back to the conference room.

Sam ducked into the back of the rented panel van to avoid being seen as Nathan and the man with him pulled out of the driveway and quickly drove past. Several minutes passed before Sam risked a look – being caught at this stage would ruin very carefully orchestrated plans.

Seeing no other movement from any other house in the vicinity, Sam smiled.

Showtime.

Sam retrieved the messenger bag packed with very specific tools. Once its strap was comfortably cross-body to leave both hands free, Sam exited the back of the van and set off at a casual stroll.

Front door? No. Too much visibility from the street…

Sam purposely walked past the house to get a good look at the side and noticed a sturdy-looking wooden gate that would grant access to the back of the Thomas property.

There we go.

Sam continued down the sidewalk at a relaxed pace, reached the end of the block, then turned around and walked back toward the target, glancing around occasionally to see if anyone else was in sight. Satisfied that the coast was clear, Sam abruptly left the sidewalk and hurried down the north side of the house toward the gate.

The gate's lock proved no match for the tools Sam had brought along, and in a few moments it yielded. Sam worked the gate open enough to shimmy through, then closed it again.

Three steps forward brought Sam to a panel box attached to the home's exterior. With a few well-placed snips, the alarm system was rendered useless. Sam returned the heavy-duty wire cutters to the messenger bag and crept forward to the northeastern corner of the ranch-style home where a large, well-maintained backyard came into view. To Sam's immediate left were two windows spaced roughly thirty feet apart.

Sam peeked through the first window and noted that the master bedroom was empty. The second window, however, revealed a sleeping child, and Sam retreated to the master bedroom's window.

Once the screen had been carefully cut away, Sam shoved against the window's frame, pleasantly surprised when it slid up easily. Slowly, the window was raised as quietly as possible until there was enough space for Sam to slither through.

That accomplished, Sam withdrew a gun from the messenger bag before crossing the room to the door. Hearing no one, Sam eased the door open and stepped out into the hallway.

***

Bella and Faith sat at the kitchen table talking.

"I really hope they're successful," Faith said before she took another sip of tea. "The not knowing has got to be stressful."

"It is," Bella admitted. "But if push comes to shove, Nathan will send me and Charlie north for a while."

Her face turned wistful.

"I wish Uncle Max were still alive," she confessed. "He'd be working behind the scenes to keep Nathan safe. I'm frightened for Charlie but even more for Nathan. He sets his sights on something and goes after it and gives no thoughts to his own safety at all."

Faith shrugged. "Wish I could tell you different, but he's always been that way."

"Yes, he most certainly has," came an unfamiliar voice from the doorway.

Startled, Bella and Faith both leapt up from their seats to confront the intruder. Bella's eyes went wide as the first tranquilizer dart struck Faith in the neck. Horrified, she gasped as her sister-in-law crumpled to the kitchen floor.

"Who are..." she started to ask but stopped short as a sharp pain pierced her upper left chest. Bella looked down at the dart protruding from her body, then stumbled backward and landed hard in her chair.

Their assailant walked slowly forward and smirked down at her as she struggled to try to stand up again.

"Who... who *are* you..." Bella managed to whisper before she lost consciousness.

The moment Nathan and Rick walked into the conference room Lizzie rushed toward them.

"You need to see this," she declared as she thrust a sheaf of papers at Nathan.

He took them and scanned the first few pages, then stopped and looked at her.

"Seriously?"

"Yep," she confirmed. "And I printed out a few pictures to show the front desk clerks at the hotel for confirmation."

"Smart. Let's gear up and head that way."

"Not without this, you don't," the director said as he entered the room. "Here's the warrant you asked for. We got lucky. Judge Bennett happens to be working today."

He turned to Rick.

"You have a sidearm?"

"Not with me," Rick replied. "Besides, I figured I'd let your team go in first anyway. I'm only tagging along in case a hack or two is needed."

"You should still be armed," the director told him. "Have the boys hook you up with a weapon as well as body armor."

"No need," Nathan interjected. "I'll give him my backup piece."

The director nodded his approval.

"I've assigned two other agents to this. They're waiting downstairs for you."

"Yes, sir. Let's get moving," Nathan said to Lizzie and Rick.

The half-hour ride over to the hotel was tense and silent.

Once the two-car caravan arrived at the hotel, Lizzie and Nathan took point and approached the front desk. The woman behind the counter smiled at them.

"Good morning. How can I help you?"

"We're looking for someone. Do you recognize this person?" Lizzie began and handed over two pictures.

"I'm sorry, I'm afraid I can't disclose any information about our guests," the woman replied.

Nathan showed her his badge, then opened the manila folder he'd brought along and handed her some papers.

"We have a warrant to search the room this individual is staying in," he explained. "Your cooperation is appreciated."

"Oh, my," the woman exclaimed as she scanned the documents then handed them back to him and looked down again at the pictures Lizzie had set on the countertop.

"Yes, sir, absolutely. I do recognize that person. One moment."

A few keystrokes later, she looked up at them again.

"Room 202, registered under the name Sam Thannato. The elevators are just over there to the left."

"Thanks," Nathan replied, then turned to the two additional agents the director had provided for him.

"You two take the stairs. We'll take the elevator. Standard approach," he instructed, and they nodded before they hustled to get into position.

He turned back to the desk clerk.

"Can you please accompany us? We'll need access to the room, and I'd rather not break down the door."

"I can't leave my desk, but I can send our head of maintenance with you. He has a master key," she replied, and dialed a four-digit number.

"Tobias? Heather. Can you come to the front desk please?"

A few moments later a tall, lanky man appeared.

"Tobias, this is Agent Thomas with the FBI," Heather explained. "They have a warrant to search 202. Can you let them in, please?"

"Certainly. Right this way, folks."

As they entered the elevator, Nathan said, "When we get up there, it's best if you knock and identify yourself as maintenance, then hand me your key and step aside."

"No worries, Agent Thomas. I know the drill," Tobias answered with a grin. "This ain't the first hotel I've worked where a raid went down. Granted, they weren't as uptown as this one, but...".

After a few tense moments, they verified that room 202's occupant had already left the building. But Nathan's jaw dropped wide open as he walked across the small space and looked at the wall opposite the bed. It was filled with pictures, and in every single one, Nathan's face had been circled. Interspersed with the pictures were newspaper clippings, some going back to his Virginia Trooper days, and all with his name highlighted each time it appeared.

"Sweet Lord," Rick muttered under his breath as he took his place by Nathan's side. "Someone's got it bad for you, brother."

"Seems like," Nathan ground out between clenched teeth.

"If you think *that's* creepy, wait until you read this," Lizzie offered, and extended one gloved hand out to him.

He took the spiral notebook from her grasp and flipped through some pages.

"Um.... *wow*," he stammered, and blushed bright red at one passage.

Rick read over his shoulder and his eyebrows raised.

"Wow, indeed."

"There are seven more notebooks just like that one," Lizzie chimed in, and directed their attention over to the tiny wooden desk in one corner of the room.

"Are you surprised by this?" Rick asked him.

"Definitely," Nathan said. "I had no idea at all, to be honest. Why now, after all this time?"

"Finish reading the printouts I gave you earlier and you'll see why," Lizzie prompted.

A low whistle from the doorway caused all three of them to turn and look.

"Well, that explains why housekeeping service was refused all week," Tobias chimed in, and pointed at the wall as he approached. "This guest has been adamant that our staff leave clean towels and sheets out in the hallway rather than entering the room. I thought maybe it was just a case of OCD or something."

"I'll take a look at the laptop," Rick announced, and worked his way over to the desk to begin the task of reviewing the hard drive's contents.

A long moan from somewhere to Bella's left worked its way down into her forced sleep and brought her back to the surface. Each eyelid seemed to weigh a ton, and she blinked slowly, once, twice, before she managed to get them to stay open.

"Faith?" she rasped as she turned her head to the left.

"I'm here," Faith mumbled.

"What happened?" Bella asked as she tried to sit up and found that she couldn't move – her arms had been zip tied behind her back, and her feet bound together at the ankles. "Where's Charlie?"

"He's fine," she heard someone say, and she whipped her head to the right toward the voice, then closed her eyes and took deep breaths through her nose at the sudden wave of nausea that overtook her.

When she opened her eyes again, she realized she was staring at the living room ceiling. A glance to her left confirmed Faith was still beside her.

Bella rolled her head to the right again, much more slowly this time, and her heart leapt into her throat. The intruder was sitting on the edge of the couch, one arm tightly wrapped around a wide-eyed and whimpering Charlie, while the other was extended outward and pointing a gun at them.

"Good. You're awake," their assailant announced. "Now we just need Nathan here. But I think we'd better use your phone, Bella. Just to make sure he answers."

"You harm my husband or my child in any way and I will kill you," Bella seethed.

"As if. You're tied up on the floor, *princess*," came the sarcastically snarled retort. "And you can behave, or you can be shot, it's your choice. I really don't give a damn either way because this isn't about you. It's about me and Nathan."

"What are you gonna do? You gonna dart me again?" Bella challenged.

The intruder smirked, then lifted the gun enough to point it at the wall and squeeze the trigger. Bella and Faith both flinched, and Charlie wailed at the echo of the live and lethal round leaving the chamber.

"You thought I wouldn't bring *real* firepower?"

Bella swallowed hard as her eyes locked with Charlie's.

"It's okay, baby," she crooned. "I need you to be still and quiet, okay?"

"O...kay...," Charlie said on a tearful exhale, and sniffled.

"Enough of this," the stranger intoned, and stood, one arm tightening around a squirming Charlie.

"Come on, little one. You're my insurance that your mommy and your aunt won't try anything stupid. How about we call Daddy now?"

Chapter Twenty-Three

"Hey, honey," Nathan said when he answered his cellphone.

"Hey, yourself," he heard someone purr, and the hair on the back of his neck stood on end.

"Where's my wife?" he growled.

"We're waiting at home for you, darling," came the cryptic reply. "Me, and Bella, and your sister Faith, and your sweet little boy. Matter of fact, I've got Charlie right here with me. Charlie, wanna say hi to Daddy?"

Nathan began to tremble as he heard his toddler say, "Home now, Daddy. Home now," in a shaky voice that told Nathan he'd been crying.

"Now you listen here..."

"No, *you* listen," the mysterious caller said. "If you don't want them hurt, you'd better get your ass home. We have a lot to talk about, you and me. So don't keep me waiting – and come alone unless you want this to end badly."

He started to protest but the call disconnected.

"Rick. Lizzie. With me," he yelled as he dashed out of the hotel room.

"What's going on?" an alarmed Lizzie asked as she scrambled to keep up with him.

"My family," was all Nathan could blurt out, shaking with rage and fear as he headed for the stairwell.

"At your house?" she asked, and he nodded.

"Radio it in," Rick urged as they hustled down the stairs and out to Nathan's car.

"Can't. No cops or they'll get hurt. I have to go in alone."

"Like hell you do. You have us - and we have active comms at our disposal," Lizzie announced in a calm, firm tone as she took control of planning their approach.

"Here's what we're going to do. You're going to drop us off a half-block away, and you're going to turn your earpiece back on before you leave the car. Rick and I will work our way around to the back of the house and I will let you know when we're in position."

"Works for me," Nathan gritted as he turned the key, yanked the transmission into gear and stomped the accelerator.

Lizzie swiveled her head to look over her shoulder at Rick in the back seat.

"Can you pick a lock?"

"I've never tried."

"That's okay, because I can," she confirmed. "And their patio door has a simple one. I should be able to get us in quickly."

Fifteen minutes later, Nathan abruptly pulled the car over to the curb.

"Give us a five-minute head start, then go to your house. Comms active," Lizzie reminded him before she bailed out of the car, and he reached up to his left ear and activated the earpiece, then nodded to his teammate and his brother-in-law.

"See you in a bit," Rick said. "We'll get them out safely, Nathan, I promise."

With that, he too climbed out of the car, shut the door, and tapped the roof twice.

"Come on, let's get moving," Lizzie urged, and Nathan watched as they took off at a fast jog.

The next five minutes seemed to last an eternity as Nathan waited while the only two people that could help save his family headed to their assigned positions. Finally, it was time, and Nathan slowly maneuvered the remaining half-block and turned into his driveway.

He heard Lizzie softly but clearly through his earpiece as he turned off the motor.

"We're in back. Master bedroom window is open. Rick will be coming in that way. I'm heading toward the patio door."

"Roger. I'm going in," he replied to her, moving his mouth as little as possible in the event he was being watched from the living room window.

He took a deep breath, exited the vehicle, and walked up to the front porch, then opened the front door and stepped into his living room.

"Close the door, would you? Less distractions that way," the person holding his family hostage directed, and Nathan never broke eye contact as he obliged.

"Been a long time, Celeste," he said. "You mind telling me what the hell you think you're doing?"

"I deserve your full attention after what we shared," the petite blonde snarled, and snuggled Charlie even closer to her body.

"After what we *shared*?" Nathan said incredulously. "We were study partners at the academy for two weeks. What exactly is it that you think we shared, other than homework notes?"

"No! You know we had a connection, Nathan. Why are you denying it? We're meant to be together. This child should be *ours*, not yours and *hers*," Celeste sneered, waving her pistol in Bella's direction. "You said you loved me. We even got matching tattoos, remember?"

Nathan took a step forward with both hands raised.

"Celeste, I don't have any tattoos. I have *never* had a tattoo. I don't know who you're thinking of or why you're here, but whatever it is you're talking about, you have the wrong guy."

Charlie began to fidget in her arms.

"Stop wiggling, you little brat!" she snapped, and adjusted her grip on him so that he was now facing away from Nathan and looking over her shoulder.

Lizzie popped the lock as quietly as she could and eased the back door of Nathan and Bella's home open wide enough to slide through. Her weapon drawn and ready, she crept stealthily across the tile flooring toward the living room, where she could hear Nathan talking to a woman.

Suddenly the uninvited guest appeared in the doorway ahead of her, but luckily the woman was facing the living room, not the kitchen.

Lizzie could see Charlie's pale, scared face over the woman's shoulder. He saw Lizzie and his eyes went wide. She quickly made a shushing motion to him, and the child nodded once, very slowly.

Meanwhile, the woman who was clutching Charlie to her as a human shield was talking more and more loudly, arguing her point to Nathan. From her vantage point Lizzie could see Nathan, and she knew that given the circumstances he'd do nothing to alert the crazed woman holding his child to Lizzie's presence.

Dammit. I don't have a clear shot. I can't risk hitting Charlie.

She crept to within ten feet of the woman who was shouting to the rooftops that if she couldn't have Nathan, no one could, and Lizzie's heart plummeted as the woman suddenly raised her gun and fired, striking Nathan in the chest.

As Nathan fell backward, Charlie began to kick and scream. Mid-meltdown the toddler leaned his upper body as far back as he could. His captor pivoted with him, trying to keep her balance and him under control, and noticed Lizzie.

She raised her gun to shoot at Lizzie when Charlie suddenly flung himself forward again - and headbutted the woman clutching at him on the bridge of her nose just before she pulled the trigger.

Her eyes watering, the intruder shrieked and dropped both the child and her pistol to bring her hands up to her face. The shot she'd taken at Lizzie went wide, hitting Lizzie in the fleshy part of her upper left arm.

Charlie landed on his feet and made a beeline for Bella. The moment that he was safely out of the way, Lizzie returned fire, sending three rounds into the attacker's upper chest. The impact hurled the blonde backward and she landed hard on her back on the living room floor. Lizzie immediately rushed forward to kick her weapon out of reach, then straddled her prone form to ensure she couldn't harm anyone else.

"Nathan! You good?" Lizzie called out as she kept her gun's muzzle firmly in contact with the center of the blonde's forehead.

"Yeah," he managed on a groan as he sat up.

He unzipped and removed his jacket, then pulled off his bullet-proof vest.

"Damn, that hurt. I think I've got some cracked ribs," he wheezed.

"That's a safe bet. Her gun's what? A .40 caliber? That will break some bones for sure. Call an ambulance," Lizzie said.

"Already on it," Rick remarked, phone to his ear, as he joined them from the hallway and quickly crossed the room to cut away Bella and Faith's bonds while he rattled off the address to the emergency services operator.

"Is everyone else all right?" Lizzie asked.

Nathan crawled the short distance to his wife and child.

"Charlie's got a goose egg on his forehead, but other than that I think he's okay," Nathan reported, and wrapped his arms around Bella and Charlie.

"Lizzie, is she..." Bella asked, pointing at the woman Lizzie had pinned to the floor.

"Bitch has a vest on. I can feel it," came Lizzie's sharp retort. "She's probably got a broken nose, and maybe a mild concussion. But otherwise, she's physically healthy and primed for arrest and trial, trust me – unless she does anything else stupid."

Lizzie looked down at the blonde she was sitting on.

"You gonna do anything else stupid? Because I'd love nothing better than to pull the trigger again right now."

Her captive's eyes bulged in terror in response, but the blonde did not move or speak.

Meanwhile, Rick helped Faith to her feet and then enveloped her in a hug.

"I'm fine, honey, I promise. Let's help Lizzie. That's a lot of blood," Faith observed, and pulled away to rush into the kitchen for a clean dishtowel to try and staunch the bleeding.

Hearing Faith's declaration, Nathan glanced over at Lizzie and frowned when he noticed Lizzie's left arm steadily raining bright red droplets onto the hardwood floor.

"You're hit? Why didn't you tell me you were hit?" he asked his teammate.

Lizzie shrugged, then winced at the pain in her left arm.

"Through-and-through. It stings but I'll be fine," she quipped with a wan smile, then tilted her head and listened.

"The calvary's here. Someone get the door."

Within ten minutes, Lizzie's humor had fled.

"It's a flesh wound," Lizzie grumbled, and tried without success to yank her arm away from the paramedic.

"And that's your opinion. But the truth is, you've got a pretty serious hole in your arm," the man barked back, "and you can hold still, or I can and will strap you down."

She growled and stared at Nathan standing in her line of sight just outside the ambulance's open doors.

"Could have at least let me walk out here unaided. I'm not crippled, you know," she snarled, which earned her a grin from her boss.

"Let them tend to you. Please?" he asked.

"What about you?" she challenged, then looked at the paramedic.

"Hey, *he's* probably got a few cracked ribs, at least. You need to work on him too."

"My partner will be checking him here shortly," the man reassured her. "Now please hold still."

Rick came into her view.

"I'm driving Faith to the hospital. She seems fine, but I want to make sure there's no lasting effects from the tranquilizer," he told them both.

"And I am taking Bella and Charlie in, too," Nathan assured him.

"Who's gonna stay here? We can't leave your house open like that," Lizzie protested.

"No worries, Agent Zimmerman," the director said as he came to a stop beside Nathan. "I'll stay until the evidence crews are done, and I'll lock up. And after that, I'll come up to the hospital to personally escort Celeste Monsill to a jail cell."

"Where is she? Where's my *wife*?" Lizzie heard someone yell and closed her eyes in frustration.

"Guys, tell me you didn't panic my husband over a simple through-and-through."

"No, but we sure as hell weren't about to try to hide the fact that you got shot from him, either," Rick retorted, then stumbled back as Donny shoved his way past him and into the ambulance.

"Jesus. You all right?" he asked before he leaned forward, took her face in his hands, and kissed her.

"Breathe, baby. I'm good," she reassured him, and raised her right hand to stroke his cheek. "I'm fine."

"You look awfully pale," he observed, his eyebrows arched in worry.

"She's lost a lot of blood," the paramedic chimed in. "And if I could get her to stop fighting me, I could get a line started to help deal with that."

"Cooperate, please," Donny told her gently as he touched his forehead to hers.

"Ugh. *Fine.*"

Forty-five minutes into their arrival at Harris Methodist's emergency room, Rick and Nathan met in the hallway to compare notes.

"Charlie has a mild concussion," Nathan revealed. "I'm not surprised, given the size of that knot on his head. But Bella's fine. Whatever kind of tranquilizer that was, it seems to have metabolized quickly."

"They said the same thing about Faith," Rick confirmed. "What about you?"

"Two cracked ribs and a big ugly bruise, and other than wrapping a tight bandage around me there's not much they can do about any of it."

"Ouch. Any updates on Lizzie?"

"I haven't checked on her yet, but I was about to."

Donny came strolling up.

"How are Faith, Bella, and Charlie?"

"Good, overall," Nathan responded. "Charlie's got a mild concussion, is all. We got lucky."

"We got *really* lucky," Rick confirmed. "And when we get everyone out of here, we'll have to celebrate. How is Lizzie doing?"

When Donny didn't answer right away, Nathan took a second look at him and noticed his dazed expression.

"What's wrong?" Nathan asked. "Did something happen to Lizzie?"

"You could say that," Donny managed. "They want to do surgery on her arm, but she's refusing."

"Why?"

"Two reasons. One, because she didn't want to miss any updates on Charlie and the girls. And two…".

Donny paused, then grinned from ear to ear.

"Because we just found out Lizzie's five weeks pregnant. The anesthesiologist is on his way down to talk to us about options that are safest for the baby."

He accepted congratulations from them both, then quipped, "Guess I'd better get back in there. It will help calm her if she knows that Bella, Faith, and Charlie are okay."

Donny turned and took three steps, then turned back toward them with a radiant smile.

"I'm gonna be a dad. Can you believe it? I'm gonna be a *dad*."

Epilogue

Two days later, Nathan and Rick sat across from the director in his office.

"Cesar Nelson has another death attributed to him," Nathan told his boss. "Evidence found in his Land Rover led to the discovery of another body here in Dallas — a woman named Noelle Zypher. She was strangled to death in her apartment."

"What evidence?"

"A complete copy of Annie's rental paperwork," Nathan explained. "From when Ben added her to his lease. Ms. Zypher worked as the receptionist in the apartment complex's leasing office. We think Nelson convinced her to give him a copy of Annie's files, then killed her."

"I've reviewed security footage from that location," Rick offered. "And just like all the other murder sites, the security feed at Ms. Zypher's apartment building experienced a significant disruption."

"Sounds pretty open and shut, then," the director mused, and Nathan nodded.

"So, about Celeste Monsill," the director began, and Nathan heaved a sigh and then winced at the twinge of pain in his ribs.

"Not much to tell, really. She started at the FBI academy the same week I did. She was a loner, didn't talk much. We wound up studying together a couple of times, and then she stopped showing up one day. I just figured she'd decided to quit the program. I had no idea they'd kicked her out until I read what Lizzie found."

"Why do you think she focused on you?" Rick asked.

Nathan ran a hand through his hair.

"I honestly have no idea. Maybe I was the only one that was nice to her."

He looked at Rick and then his boss.

"I certainly didn't do anything more than study with her, I can guarantee that."

"And I believe you," the director assured him. "Dr. Bailey called me earlier, by the way. The journal pages were an exact match to both notes left at the murder scenes and to the partially completed application. We've also got the other physical evidence collected, as well. That part of the case is solid. What's not clear is Ms. Monsill's mental state. It could very well be that her defense attorney pleads insanity. We'll just have to wait and see."

The director paused for a moment, then changed topics again.

"How are Agent Zimmerman and Hank Myers doing?"

"Lizzie was released yesterday morning," Nathan revealed. "And last I spoke with Annie, Hank's surgery went smoothly, but I haven't heard when he will be discharged yet."

A soft ping from Rick's phone caused him to glance at its screen and smile before he returned it to its holster.

"Everything okay?" a curious Nathan asked.

"Fine."

The director arched an eyebrow but didn't comment on whatever was happening with Rick. Instead, he focused on Nathan.

"And Agent Womack?"

"She came back into town last night, and she'll be here for tonight's shift as scheduled."

A rap on the door interrupted.

"Come in," the director snapped, and seemed to be as shocked as Nathan and Rick were when the DEA's Dallas branch director stepped into the room.

"I have an update that I think you'd like to know about," he said without preamble. "Estoban Cortinas was murdered late last night at his compound. From the intel we've gathered, it seems that the Cortinas cartel ran into some severe financial difficulties – so severe that their Colombian suppliers decided to take drastic action."

Nathan's boss whistled long and low, but Nathan's focus was drawn to the way that Rick shifted, almost imperceptibly, in his seat at the DEA man's news.

"Interesting. Potential fallout?" Nathan's boss asked his counterpart.

"Not known yet," the man confirmed. "But my gut tells me whatever's left of the cartel now has much bigger problems to deal with than coming after any of us."

"I appreciate the update," the FBI director said, and the DEA man nodded, then left.

"Well, then. I don't think that there is anything else to cover right now," the director announced then shifted his gaze to Rick.

"Mr. Conner, as usual, we're grateful for your assistance."

Rick inclined his head. "Thank you, sir."

They stepped out into the hallway, and the director's office door had barely closed behind them when Nathan turned to Rick.

"What did you do?" he challenged and folded his arms lightly across his chest.

"Why, whatever do you mean?" Rick replied, his voice and face projecting an innocence that made Nathan laugh out loud, which in turn made him wince in pain.

"The cartel's just *suddenly* having money trouble? I'm a lot of things, Rick, but stupid isn't one of them. Now, what did you do?"

Rick glanced around to make sure they were alone in the hallway, then leaned in close to his brother-in-law.

"Don't ask me about that. It's best if you don't."

"Why?"

"Two words – *plausible deniability*," Rick whispered solemnly, his eyes never breaking contact with Nathan's.

"Seriously?"

Rick raised an eyebrow in response.

"Holy shit. You're a rock star, did you know that?" Nathan whispered back, and Rick grinned.

"I've been told that a time or two, yes."

"Man, I would move heaven and earth to get you on the team full-time," Nathan lamented as they resumed their walk to the elevator. "Are you sure you won't change your mind about that?"

"Well," Rick said but didn't elaborate, and as the elevator doors opened he stepped inside. Nathan, still standing on the eighth floor, shot an arm up and out to stop the doors from closing between them and waited.

"Well, what?"

"Well, Nathan, you've talked me into it. Yes. I'll join your team as a full-timer. Does me starting on Monday work for you? Because I really need the rest of this week to line out a new schedule for the bookstore," he announced.

He grinned again when Nathan, jaw hanging open, was so stunned by the response that he lowered his arm and let the elevator doors slide to a close.

Author's Note

Thank you so, so much for going on the *Vital Secrets* journey with me! I hope you enjoyed following along with Nathan Thomas and his team in their adventures. Now, they're going to take a well-deserved break for a while.

Join my *spam-free* newsletter to stay updated on the latest news and events!

SUBSCRIBE

Follow me on BookBub

Follow me on Goodreads

Follow me on Facebook

COMING SOON (2023):

The *Raven's Path* Series

Also by D.F. Hart

Vital Secrets

Mystery, Suspense and Thriller written as D.F. Hart

Book of Secrets

List of Secrets

Web of Secrets

Path of Secrets

Carnival of Secrets

House of Secrets

End of Secrets

Vital Secrets, Volume 1-3

Vital Secrets, Volume 4-6

Raven's Path - Coming in 2023

Mystery, Suspense and Thriller written as D.F. Hart

Raven's Rise

Raven's Attack

One Last Gift – An Anthology by James N. Richardson (D.F. Hart, Editor & Publisher)

About the Author

D.F. Hart resides in Texas. Her favorite authors include Frederick Forsyth, Ken Follett, and J.D. Robb. Other interests include hidden object and puzzle games—she loves a good mystery storyline!

Of writing, she says: "It's a lot of work, but also an escape. A lot of tears and sweat go into a story, building believable characters, shaping the plot so that the reader can't wait to turn the page. Sometimes I'll wake up at 3 a.m. with that perfect line that escaped me earlier in the day running through my head. But it's worth it. And the brilliant part is, you get to create a little universe of your own. Anything can happen; there are no limits."

She happily pens mysteries and thrillers under D.F. Hart, and contemporary and suspenseful romance as Faith Hart.

9 781952 008344